The Goddess Documents

Trudi L. White

Prologue

It was every kind of quiet. At least that's how it felt to the two little girls. Six years old and sneaking around in the middle of the night, they were terrified. Slowly they crept down the stairs, first to the main level of the house, then through the kitchen. As they approached the cellar, they almost turned back. They felt very brave, and very terrified at the same time.

Maybe there was an eerie chill in the air, maybe it was just the flimsy cotton nightgowns they wore. Whatever it was, both girls shivered profusely. Bravely they pushed forward.

The easy part was over. As they stood in the cold dark kitchen near the door that opened to the basement, they felt as if the challenge would be impossible to meet.

The old-fashioned crystal doorknob seemed to wink in the light of the full moon. Just that light alone, almost startled them into turning back.

Finally, the braver of the two girls reached out, turned the knob and opened the door. Just as the door opened they saw a flickering light and heard the steady chanting. The old staircase creaked as they stepped together onto the first

step down. They linked arms to support each other in a show of bravery. Just as they were about to brave the next stair, there was a loud bang.

They jumped apart as fast as they could and ran up and out through the kitchen and living room. They ran up the stairs to the four-poster bed where they crawled under the covers and sat gaping at each other in wide-eyed fear.

CHAPTER ONE

Bri could not believe what was happening to her. Here she sat with copies of the ancient scrolls in her hand. Well, they weren't scrolls now but she was told that they had been at one time. She had been invited to be an apprentice to a high priestess. 24 hours ago she was just a woman feeling stuck in life. Stuck in her job. Stuck in her relationship. Stuck in life. She had not a clue of how to change. So she had prayed. She had prayed desperately for guidance and help. They say that when the student is ready the teacher appears. Even though she had prayed, Bri didn't feel ready. Not for this kind of teaching. She stared down at the papers on her lap again, amazed at the title; "The Daughters of Inanna."

She was so afraid to open them that she actually trembled. So Bri stared. After awhile, she replayed the meeting in her mind for what seemed like the hundredth time.

Bri had been called to Windmere House to meet with Anne-Marie Brody as a potential client. There had been some pretense about drawing up a will. Although she was an attorney, Bri didn't normally do wills. Usually that kind of thing would have been given to another associate in the San Francisco firm where she worked. But apparently, this Mrs. Brody had asked for Bri by name.

She remembered approaching the house for the first time. Bri had been struck by the majesty of the house.

As she walked towards the house Bri couldn't help thinking how stately, elegant and beautiful it looked. The white Victorian seemed misplaced in time and space. It seemed as if it had survived a war or an earthquake, as if it had seen the worst and the best and remained standing.

Bri felt the wrought iron gate against her hand. It creaked slightly as she had imagined it would. Time seemed to slow as she walked up the sidewalk, up 12 steps to the massive door. She stood in front of a very elegant and forbidding door. It was made of mahogany and stained glass.

Bri pushed the old bell on the side of the door while she tried to make out the image in the stained glass. Before she could make sense of it, the door opened, and there stood a very old woman. She looked to be in her late 80s or 90s, but she still had a vibrant and confident air. "Stately, elegant and beautiful," flashed through Bri's mind again.

Bri admired the woman's dress. It too looked like it had survived. It was fresh and immaculate. But Bri imagined that the emerald dress had survived. It, as well as the woman, would have been perfectly comfortable in this house 150 years earlier.

Bri was ushered into the Parlor. There could be no other name for such a room. Honey brown round tables with doilies and lots of rugs were scattered around the room.

Even the rounded wooden arms of the mauve sofa echoed a feeling of times long past. Once again, Bri felt as if she had been removed from time and space.

Just as they sat down, the little wooden clock on the mantle over the fireplace chimed six times. The lights were dimmed to reflect the evening meeting.

"So good of you to come this late," the woman said in a strong, yet very quiet voice. "I would have asked you to come earlier, but I've been away."

"Well this is just fine. I'm very happy we were able to arrange this meeting at all." Bri replied.

"You do look so much the same as always," said the old woman.

Until that moment Bri had thought that the old woman had maintained all of her faculties despite her advancing years. Now she wondered.

"But we've never met before?" Bri found herself surprised by her own question.

"Well – not that you'd remember." replied Mrs. Brody.

Things only got stranger from there. Half an hour later, Bri was staring at Anne-Marie Brody with an open mouth.

"So, I'm supposed to believe I'm one of these Daughters of Inanna, a secret society of women that goes back thousands of years? And this "honor" was passed on to me by my mother who died when I was only six years old?" asked Bri.

"Well, yes Dear," said Anne-Marie Body. "Haven't you ever felt you were different from other girls?"

"Who doesn't?"

"You're different in the way you know some things. Just know. That's called direct knowing. You're also different in the way you decide things and then make them happen. I'll bet you that when you decided to be a lawyer, the doors just opened and it was done without any second guess or hesitation on your part?"

"I'm decisive. That makes me a Daughter of Inanna? Most of the professional women I know are decisive. We have to be in order to make it."

"Yes dear, but if you ask them, most will tell you they've had second thoughts. Most women automatically question their intuition and consequently their decisions. That just isn't the case with you is it?"

Bri hesitated, and then answered, "That still doesn't prove anything."

"Dear, if you will just stop and listen to your Inner Self for a moment, you won't need any proof."

"This is where my direct knowing is supposed to kick in. I'm sorry I just can't buy into any of this. And I'm certainly not about to join some cult that worships an ancient goddess."

"Dear, we don't worship the goddess. Our women come to us with all their own spiritual beliefs. We don't seek to disrupt that. We allow for growth into a deeper understanding of the nature of spirituality. Inanna is more of a guide for us. We respect her. We honor her. We draw strength from her. But we don't worship her."

Bri felt her guard start to slip a bit. She recovered quickly.

"Still this whole thing sounds crazy to me. The privilege of this training will cost me a mere...?" Bri waited to see if the sophisticated older woman slipped into con man mode.

"Oh no, this won't cost you anything. We plan ahead for our Daughters' education. Your mother paid the fee while you were still a baby. Our investment team is able to take a relatively small amount and invest it to pay for your entire training by the time you're 30. Any remainder will of course revert to you, although many of our women choose to invest the additional in the organization."

Anne-Marie paused while she took a sip of tea.

"You wouldn't be here now if you hadn't been asking for this at some deep level of your soul. When you ask for something the universe always answers."

"Why don't you have tea with Diana next week," she continued. "Diana runs the house and the United States organization. She knew your mother quite well. Here take this too; it's a little reading material. Get to know a little more about what I'm talking about."

Bri took the documents and walked out. The meeting had been over before she could find out more about this Diana and how she knew her mother. Bri had, however, agreed to meet Diana for tea. She thought she could find out more about her mother that way.

Now as she sat with the documents in front of her, Bri wondered how she got here. How she could feel so hopeless and alone. She wasn't alone though. She had friends. She had her boyfriend, Joseph. Being a good-looking professional African-American woman, she received a great deal of male attention in addition to Joseph. She had a great job by most standards.

Then why did she feel as if she were acting out a part? Bri felt trapped. Trapped in a life that looked so perfect on the surface. How could something that looked so wonderful feel so binding? She had always dreamed of fulfillment, of finding her purpose in life. She wanted desperately to wake up in the morning, excited about what lay ahead. But when she woke she always knew what to expect. She always knew exactly what she was going to do that day. What was prescribed according to the rules she'd chosen to live by. The number of children she would have some day had been the only real mystery in her life.

Now there was a new mystery, a new sense of excitement. She felt Windmere House calling her. She felt the call of the Daughters of Inanna. And now she recognized the call of her very soul.

Bri had been surprised that so much of what Anne-Marie told her had just felt true

Bri picked up the documents and started to read.

CHAPTER TWO

The next week, Bri eagerly kept her appointment with Diana. After introducing themselves to each other, Diana explained a little about the Daughters of Inanna and the training. Bri learned that the papers she had been given weren't actually "The Goddess Documents", but writings that had been done by the Daughters over the years.

"Of course the training doesn't come without responsibilities," explained Diana.

"What kind of responsibilities?" asked Bri.

"We help promising young women when they are floundering."

"How does that work?" asked Bri.

"Remember when you were 15? You were having a rough time. You missed your mother so much, and you were having trouble adjusting to high school."

"How do you know about that?" asked Bri.

"I got full reports from Lydia Day."

"She was my homeroom teacher!"

"Yes, and she's also a Daughter. Lydia has always

loved helping young women so much, that's why she became a teacher," mused Diana. "Anyway, those long talks the two of you had really helped restore your self-confidence didn't they?"

"I was not doing well in school until then. She helped me find the debate club, where I made friends. It really boosted my confidence. I don't think I would have made it to college, let alone law school, if it hadn't been for Mrs. Day."

"Yes, and that's only part of the story."

"What do you mean?"

"You'll understand once you're in the program. I have to go now or I'll be late for another meeting."

"What a cryptic response," thought Bri as she picked up her bag to go.

They met again a few days later after Bri had a chance to do a little more reading and let some of the ideas soak in for a while.

Bri was full of questions at their next meeting.

"So what you do is help young women achieve their dreams. Isn't that a bit like being a Fairy Godmother?" Bri asked cynically.

"Oh we haven't been called that in generations. But to tell you the truth, I always liked the romance of thinking that way," explained Diana.

"Fairy Godmothers? But isn't that sort of silly and trivial?"

"Everyone needs a Fairy Godmother from time to time dear."

"You're kidding, right? I'm supposed to go into training to be a Fairy Godmother?"

"Just like you needed Lydia Day, other women need someone who will believe in them, unconditionally, someone who can see our strengths when we're too confused to see clearly."

"We're the Daughters of Inanna. Not that there's anything wrong with Fairy Godmothers, mind you." Diana looked off into space and began to talk, as if to no one in particular.

"We all need a Fairy Godmother sometimes," she said again. "Not to magically improve us or lift us up out of our circumstances. The real magic of the Fairy Godmother is in the mirror she holds up for us to look into.

The mirror shows us the possibilities of our Selves and our lives. It shows us who we really are and what we can become.

The Fairy Godmother never brings us what we don't have. She doesn't change us. She doesn't even suggest that there is anything wrong with the way we are. She just knows the truth.

The Fairy Godmother works with what is present. In Cinderella, she transformed the girl's ragged dress into a ball gown. The Fairy Godmother enhanced what was already there.

She brought forth a different aspect of what was present. The Fairy Godmother knew with absolute certainty that what Cinderella saw was not the whole truth. The Fairy Godmother knew that in a different form the dress Cinderella was already wearing would be perfect for the ball.

Notice that Cinderella was already beautiful, charming, intelligent and graceful. She just couldn't see it herself. The Godmother didn't need to enhance that or Cinderella's wit and charm. Cinderella just needed the confidence of all the trappings. Once her confidence was bolstered by the dress, the coach and all of the accessories, Cinderella let her own inner beauty shine through. So, she was able to allow herself to win the prince. She had everything it took. She always had it.

The prince is of course only a symbol. A symbol of a young woman's heartfelt dream. Today, it could be a family, a career or a simple desire to help in the world and feel fulfilled.

That's what we all need sometimes. Someone to truly look at us. Someone to see our strength and beauty. Someone to see our true selves. Then we in turn can act as a mirror to another who doesn't see so clearly.

Most of us need the Fairy Godmother to serve as that mirror. Once we see what's really inside, our confidence builds and we demonstrate who we really are. Once our self-doubt is removed, we no longer hesitate to follow our hearts. In our hearts we find the truth and beauty of who we are. Then we truly have something to give to the world.

That's the reality of it all. That's one of the big lessons we come to this life to learn. Once we are truly ourselves, when we live from the core of our Divine nature, that's all we want to do, is give. We recognize the unity of all life. But that's very difficult to do when we're blinded by day-to-day troubles.

So that's what we do. We help women find their true Divine nature. Then the world has the gift of that beauty and that truth. And our women can't wait to return the favor by passing on beauty, truth and service to the world. We don't call ourselves Fairy Godmothers, but the principle of bringing out the best in women is one of our prime reasons for existence."

CHAPTER THREE

Bri walked into her condo, dropped her briefcase in the hall and without stopping, continued on to her bedroom where she collapsed onto the bed fully dressed. Another day at work like today and she'd scream, pull out her hair and leave.

"It isn't fair," she said to herself as she lay on the bed, eyes open, facing the ceiling. "Being a lawyer was supposed to be fun. I was going to be a crusader for justice. Instead, I've turned into a negotiator for the least offensive solution for everyone involved."

Bri flashed back to the triumphant moment when she had received her letter of acceptance to Stanford Law School. She had been ecstatic. She must have walked on cloud nine for at least a week. She really didn't come down until the first day of law school. The lectures and the work that the professors had given had dampened her enthusiasm somewhat. But Bri made it through with honors.

Bri rolled over onto her stomach, thinking, "It wasn't supposed to turn out like this." Her mind wandered back to the documents and her meetings with Diana. She wondered how choosing that path could be any worse than where she was today.

That evening, Bri shared her feelings with her boyfriend, Joseph. Joseph, who seemed perfectly content with the sacrifices and compromises he made on a day-to-day basis in his own law practice, brushed her off.

"Don't worry, after this vacation we're planning, you'll come back refreshed, renewed and revitalized in your passion for the law." Joseph kissed Bri. "What about making it the Cayman Islands? We can stay at that all inclusive resort like when we were in Jamaica."

"Maybe we should postpone the trip," suggested Bri.

"Remember how nervous you were about picking up parasites in the water in Jamaica?"

"Now is not such a good time for me to be planning a vacation. "

"Don't be silly, Weatherby will gladly give you the time off. It's been over a year since you took any real time off."

"I know. It's not the time off. It's these women I told you about, the ones in the old Queen Anne Victorian. They got me started thinking about my life."

"The Caymans are a great place to think."

"No, listen to me Joseph. This is serious. Diana knew my mother really well. I would like to spend some time with her. You know my mother died when I was six. I could really have a chance to finally learn a little about her. My father just wouldn't talk about her. Then when he remarried..."

"Do you really want to get mixed up with these women? They seem a little strange to me."

"I know, but the more I get to know them, the more at home I feel. And that house... Well I don't know, it just feels as if I belong there somehow. It's like they know who I really am."

"I know who you really are. You're a beautiful, sexy, brilliant attorney, who just happens to be crazy about me." Joseph took her into his arms. He kissed her quickly before picking up his briefcase and heading out.

Bri stared out her living room window at the San Francisco Bay. She was tired playing the role of the successful attorney. She was coming to realize that being an attorney was just what she did. It had nothing to do with who she was.

CHAPTER FOUR

Bri looked around the room. The women here all seemed perfectly normal. If she had met any of them in other circumstances, she was sure she would never have guessed their secret.

The five other women at the orientation to the Daughters of Inanna training looked as if they could be accountants, homemakers or schoolteachers. In fact, one of them, Kathy, was a schoolteacher.

At the beginning of this session they had gone around and given their names and occupations, or at least their former occupations.

The woman named Sarah had particularly intrigued Bri. Sarah had apparently been doing some type of insurance work until very recently. Bri was struck by Sarah's confidence and obviously independent nature.

She wasn't sure exactly what she had expected from this small group of women however, she was surprised to find that most of them seemed strong and independent. Not the type of women who would fall in line and just take orders.

No, these women seemed informed and interested, not the type to make a suicide pact under the influence of a charismatic leader.

Bri looked around the room again to prompt the information she had about each of these women.

Dana was a good-looking woman, with striking black hair. When she introduced herself, they discovered that she worked as an office manager for a local real estate broker.

There was Kathy, a mousy sort of looking woman with straight brown hair. She was a second grade teacher. Her chino slacks and polo shirt made her look as if she was prepared for any seven-year-old challenge.

That was a big contrast from that Debra woman. Debra was dressed in a tailored skirt and blouse. She didn't look like the type to subject those manicured nails to anything that might chip their polish. Apparently she worked in a very successful family business.

Aimee was an athletic looking journalist from the Pacific Northwest, but she seemed to have a much more worldly air. She certainly didn't seem like someone who could be easily duped.

Bri was the only African-American woman besides, Oya, one of the instructors. Working in law, Bri was very used to being in the minority. She hardly even noticed it any more.

"We consider ourselves Sisters," Diana began. "In order to bond and form that Sisterhood with your class, we require that all Trainees live here at Windmere House for the six month training period. Under these circumstances we truly become Sisters. We come to know each other and depend on each other as family. Once this bond is formed with your class you will find that it easily extends to Daughters of Inanna everywhere.

There will be breaks during Christmas and Easter when you are allowed to spend the night away. Other than that, we ask that you sleep at the house. All other nights away should be approved in advance.

You will have plenty of free time and every Sunday off. However, please be aware of the 11 pm curfew. This is out of respect for the rest of the residents of the house. It's more conducive to group living if we don't have women coming and going at all hours of the night."

Bri looked around the room to see if anyone else appeared to find the rules too restrictive.

Apparently, most of the women had already been prepared for this news. Undoubtedly by their mothers who would have endured something similar. Bri was saddened that she had never had the chance to learn about the Daughters from her own mother.

Bri felt it was unfortunate that there was no time to mingle with the other women. But the information was presented strictly lecture style.

A petite brunette approached Bri as they were leaving Windmere House.

"Hi my name is Sarah. I'm so excited to be beginning training, how about you?"

"Well, yes, but what about all of those rules?" Bri asked.

"I know, but my mom says it's not so bad once you get used to it. At least we don't have any women with children in our class. I hear that can be really rough."

"I guess so."

"Hey do you want to get to know each other some before we start training?" Sarah asked.

Bri didn't let on that she wasn't yet sure that she would be training. She did, however, think it was a good idea to get to know more about the kind of people who did this sort of thing.

"That's a great idea. Let's do lunch later this week." Bri was dying to get the perspective of someone who had grown up with knowledge of the Daughters of Inanna.

"How's Saturday?"

"Great." Bri and Sarah agreed to meet at a restaurant on Fisherman's Wharf on Saturday at noon.

CHAPTER FIVE

Lunch had stretched into the late afternoon and finally to a dinner prepared by Sarah in her small apartment.

Bri was amazed at everything Sarah knew about the Daughters of Inanna. Apparently there were all sorts of ceremonies, rituals and traditions. The documents Bri had read were just the tip of the iceberg.

"How the Triad knew that the gifts would pass through the maternal line for generations to come, I don't have any idea." Sarah said in answer to one of Bri's many questions.

Apparently the Triad had come together centuries ago to form the Daughters of Inanna. One of them had rescued "The Goddess Documents" from the fires in Alexandria. She brought the other two priestesses together to form the Daughters of Inanna. Since then the documents and gifts have passed from generation to generation through the maternal line.

The Triad had set up the form in which the Daughters still existed today. Most of the ceremonies were handed directly from one generation to the next. The biggest changes involved translation to the current language of the Daughters.

"But why do we have to be thirty to begin the training?" asked Bri.

"Mom always said it was because a young woman needs time to explore the world and to discover the value of herself and her life before committing to life as a Daughter," replied Sarah.

"Committing to a life as a Daughter... you make it sound like joining a nunnery, or something." Bri said nervously.

"Oh, no, nothing like that. Obviously our mothers married and raised families. But when the Daughters call, they always return. It's in service to the Daughters, the world, and young women everywhere. Being a Daughter of Inanna is definitely a calling. I've been waiting for my turn to answer the call my entire life."

Bri was now feeling both jealous and inadequate because Sarah had been raised not only by her mother, but also with the knowledge she would one day become a Daughter.

Having lost her mother at age six, Bri had missed out on all of that. Since her father had passed on two years ago, Bri had no one to ask about why none of this part of her mother had ever been shared with her.

Bri understood now what that hole she had felt all her life had been. Her stepmother, Jules, had done her best to fill that hole by being a good mother to Bri. But now Bri understood that mothering alone could never fill the hole of her heritage as a Daughter of Inanna.

Sarah had spent the first seven years of her life after college working claims at a major insurance company. It allowed her to get a professional position and earn a comfortable living after college. Being able to have the freedom of a job that didn't tie her to a desk suited Sarah's independent spirit too. Looking at the petite brunette, you would never guess that she was a woman who lifted ladders and crawled under houses handling hurricane, tornado and earthquake claims.

Unlike Bri, Sarah had no hesitation. She had given a months notice and taken a month off in preparation to begin training. Because of her mother, Sarah had always known she'd enter the apprentice program when she turned 30. That's why she had chosen the career she had. She knew it was something she could get actively involved in, get real world experience, make a good living at and yet walk away from without any hesitation when the time came.

The people at her office had, of course, been surprised when this successful young woman had given her notice. Unlike the others, she had not spent lunch hours and happy hours griping about the company and the insurance industry. They had all thought she would be a fast riser on the corporate ladder.

Sarah had been prepared for the questions, too. She told everyone she was going to take time to discover who she was and maybe do some writing. Both things were definitely true. Sarah planned to write empowering books for women after she completed training. It would also allow her the mental stimulation she needed, as well as leave her flexibility in her schedule for assignments from the Daughters.

As Bri left Sarah's apartment, she realized that she was seriously considering becoming a Trainee. In her mind she was working out how she could manage so much time away from work.

CHAPTER SIX

The next day Bri met with Diana again. This time at Windmere House.

"Here, sit here at the desk." said Diana.

Bri sat and watched as Diana walked to the bookshelves. She brought down one heavy book after another. Some of the books appeared to be photo albums, while others, journals and scrapbooks.

"These are some of your mother's things," said Diana.

"All of this? What is all of this?" Bri asked.

"These were your mother's photos, letters, and writings for the Daughters."

Bri reached out a hand a slowly opened an album. She gasped and cried out. "But this is my mother as a child. My father said that there were only a few photos of my mother, their wedding photo, her holding me as a baby and a couple of the three of us together. He said he never knew her parents. That he knew nothing of her childhood. These are all so..." Bri gasped. "Is this my Grandmother?"

"Yes, Dear – Marian was with us for many years. She was a cornerstone in our design and development of this house as our home and sanctuary, as well as in the safety of the Goddess Documents. Her background in Egyptology helped us to develop some clever ways of safeguarding the sacred papers."

Bri sat stunned and speechless; hurt seeping in through every pore of her body.

"And Daddy knew all about this? She asked.

"He was here when they were dating, marveling at the photos of your mother as a child, amazed at some of her writings."

"And mother, why didn't she take all this? At least the photo albums - when she married and set up her own home?"

"This was like a family home to her. The place she could always come back to and rest in family and tradition. She felt this was where all this belonged. You take a couple of these. Go home. Have time with you mother."

That night, Bri had a dream. She dreamed that she was walking with her mother beside a lake. In the dream, Bri started out as a small child, and then abruptly changed to her current age.

Her mother didn't say anything in the dream, but when Bri looked in her mother's eyes she saw such incredible peace and joy. The beauty she saw when she looked at her mother was beyond anything Bri had ever seen in any photos of her. It was beyond anything she had ever seen.

As they walked, Bri couldn't help but turn her head often, to see that her mother was really there. Bri knew in her dream that her mother had passed on. But she was still very much present with Bri as they walked.

They walked on to the top of a hill. From the top of the hill, Bri could see for what seemed like miles. All that she saw was the beauty of nature and the harmony of it all. It seemed so perfect.

Bri turned and looked at her mother again. The woman she was looking at seemed completely fulfilled and at peace. Bri's mother reached out and hugged her. In that moment Bri felt more loved and protected than she ever remembered feeling in her life. She let out a deep sigh of contentment.

At that moment Bri woke up. She recalled her dream and knew at once what to do. "I want to be that peaceful and fulfilled when my life is over," she whispered to herself.

Bri wasn't sure why, but she knew she had to pursue this fully. Maybe it was seeing her mother's papers. Maybe it was the wisdom of the documents she had read. Maybe it was the dream, but somewhere inside, she knew this was the chance of a lifetime, the calling of a lifetime. Reviewing some of the documents that Diana had lent her had convinced her, finally. It was something she had to do.

She decided that she would tell her boss, Arthur, first thing in the morning. She would be requesting a leave of absence.

The training didn't begin until October, so that would give her about six weeks. She would give two weeks notice at the office. That would give her time to put things in order there and hand off her clients. Then she would have a month to herself.

Whatever this journey would be Bri was sure it would require knowing herself. Since she'd spent the last few years so buried in work she hardly had time to look in the mirror, let alone contemplate who she really was.

Yes, six weeks would be about right.

CHAPTER SEVEN

That night, she decided to tell Joseph of her decision. It wasn't as if she'd expected him to understand. Not really. However, she had expected some respect. Bri had mixed feelings as she reviewed her last encounter with Joseph.

Clearly Joseph had not been distraught about losing her; he had never professed his undying love. But his pride had suffered a tremendous blow.

"How could you choose those women, that house, over me?" he shouted.

Joseph had gone on to tell her that leaving her job and living in Windmere House was tantamount to joining a cult.

Bri was happy that her promise of confidentiality had prevented her from sharing the whole truth with Joseph. She had merely told him that she would live in the house with Sarah, Diana and Anne-Marie, while she took time to get to know herself. In order to commit fully, she had decided to tell him that the time she had allotted did not include him.

The funny thing was she was sure that Joseph wouldn't miss her one bit. No doubt he'd have a date lined up for the weekend by the time he left the gym tomorrow.

Even stranger to Bri was the thought that she wouldn't miss Joseph at all. In fact she felt a great relief to have finally put an end to this relationship, which had been pleasant, but going nowhere for the last eighteen months.

Slowly Bri pulled out her journal and began to write.

The six weeks had passed so quickly and so peacefully. Bri couldn't remember a time in her life when she felt more at ease with herself. Besides preparing her finances and her condo to do without her for a year, Bri spent the time renewing and reviewing herself. Bri found that she had an affinity for the yoga classes she had started doing four times a week. So much so, that she had developed a routine that she followed on her own on days when she didn't get to class.

Bri was surprised that she didn't feel sinful or decadent for sleeping in late and taking long naps in the afternoon. Obviously her body could use the rest. She had pushed it to the hilt for the last several years. Bri could tell by the surge in energy and life force that she felt, that sleep was just the prescription she needed for renewal.

Bri had always journaled. Reviewing her journals since college, she was amazed. In college her journals had been so full of life. She had had dreams. Ideas and creativity flowed constantly in and around her. During law school that enthusiasm and creativity had waned somewhat, but it was still present.

Bri felt really sad for the person her journals revealed her to have become in the last several years. Days consumed with work. There was little personality at all, let alone creativity coming from the woman she had become.

But now, Bri felt it again. She felt the enthusiasm. A creativity and love of life flowed right through her onto the page. She was even starting to restore her own love for herself.

Bri was grateful for the weekly lunches with Sarah to keep her focused on her goal. Everything Sarah told her convinced Bri more and more that she had made the right choice. She also felt a pull towards Sarah that she had never felt towards anyone else. She wondered if that had to do with the Daughters or was more personal than that.

Every week that passed, Bri seemed to miss Sarah more and more during their time apart. Bri was looking forward to being able to spend more time with Sarah when they moved into the house.

CHAPTER EIGHT

Bri knew from her previous visits that Windmere House was large. Now as she approached it, she realized it was enormous. She hadn't completely reconciled the fact that she would be living here yet. Bri stood for a moment on the sidewalk just appreciating the Queen Anne Victorian. She had never in her life imagined that she would live in a house with towers. She shook her head, and walked up to the door.

Diana gave Bri a tour of the first floor of Windmere House. Several rooms in the old house had been converted for modern purposes. The house now had a boardroom, a family room, and a common room, in addition to the parlor. The old library had remained, but it appeared to be outfitted with computers, state of the art lighting and wonderfully comfortable reading chairs. Diana and Anne-Marie both had private offices. In addition, there were two offices for use by visiting Daughters.

The kitchen in the house had been completely redone. Well, at least the modern conveniences anyway. It still retained its early 20th century feel with wood floors and crystal doorknobs.

When, the tour was over, Bri did not miss the fact that certain areas were apparently off-limits. There had been no explanation, regarding the purpose of several rooms. Diana had firmly explained that those were private areas.

"Helen is our housemother, she'll show you to your room," said Diana.

Bri followed Helen up the stairs. They walked down the hall and then up another flight of stairs. Bri's room was on the third floor. Once they entered, she went immediately to the window to look out. Wow, what an amazing view of the city!" Bri said as she turned to face Helen.

"Yes, I picked out this room special for you. It was the same room your mother stayed in. She loved it. Of course it's been painted and remodeled since then. But I always feel like a person's energy stays where they have lived, don't you?"

"Umm, I never really thought about it. You knew my mother?"

"Oh yes, we were in the same class together. I had a room right down the hall from Aurelia. Now, I'm downstairs. I remember you too, Bri. You were quite an active little girl, such a bright mind, and a keen curiosity. I knew you would be back here some day to train. Yes, I knew it. Not all of the daughters of the Daughters return you know. But I could tell by your light and energy that you would be back."

"It's funny to hear you call her Aurelia. On the rare occasions that my father talked about her, he called her Lia. I knew her name was Aurelia, but I never heard any one call her that."

"That's funny," replied Helen. "Your father, Vic, is the only one I hear ever call her Lia."

"Am I very much like my mother?"

"In some ways you're so much like her it's scary. But, you're your own person all right. I could see that when you were just a baby. You were born just two and a half years after your mother was initiated. There's the bell, it'll be another Trainee, I suppose."

Bri felt like she'd entered a new world in more ways than one. It was strange to suddenly enter a world where everyone knew her mother. For years, there had been a vacuum of information. Now she was bombarded. She turned back to the window and looked out over the city.

Bri was a little disoriented as she unpacked her things at Windmere house. She felt a little bit like she was back in college, moving into the dorm. She still thought it was strange that all seven Trainees had to live in the house for the six month period of training. She'd have been a little worried that Joseph was right about the cult thing if it were not for her conversations with Sarah. Sarah was obviously her own woman.

Although her mother was a Daughter, Sarah had never lived in the house. She came eagerly to participate in the training. After getting to know Sarah over the past few weeks, Bri could honestly say she'd never met a woman who was more of an independent thinker.

There were seven of them sitting around the conference room table, seven potential new Daughters of Inanna, anyway. Standing at the front of the room stood

Diana - the Training Coordinator, Mary or Mother as they called her and Oya, additional instructors in the training. Anne-Marie also stood there as part of the opening of this year's class of Daughters of Inanna.

As Bri looked around the room, she was struck by the beauty of one of the other Trainees. Her name was Jessie and she was absolutely stunning, with her auburn hair and green eyes. She had not been at the orientation, Bri noted.

Bri looked again, still trying to take in Jessie's beauty. Unfortunately it appeared that Jessie recognized her own physical beauty all too much. Bri wasn't sure if she was fantasizing about her role as a Daughter and the gifts and training involved, but she could almost swear she could sense how Jessie's knowledge and pride in her outer beauty diminished the light of the inner beauty of her soul.

Anne-Marie opened the training. She began with introductions of the instructors. Then she launched straight into the background of the Daughters of Inanna.

"Inanna is our principal goddess. She sets the standard for us and offers us empowerment and protection. But we believe in many goddesses. We believe there is a realm where the goddesses dwell. In this realm they live eternally. Some would say that the goddesses dwell on the same realm as angels. We believe that Inanna, like the other goddesses, is available to us now and forever."

Anne-Marie went on to talk about the history and traditions of the Goddess Inanna. To Bri it felt like Anne-Marie was telling a very old and very sacred story.

After a short break, the women came back and Anne-Marie began again.

"One of our foundational principles in the Daughters is intentional living. For us this means stepping out of a world in which most people live by default. We can either choose the lives we want to lead or let life happen to us.

This doesn't mean we have to plan out each moment of our lives. It doesn't mean we need to try to control situations or outcomes. For us it's more of setting a course. Choosing to live a conscious life. Making decisions about the moment we're in now.

Most importantly it's about choosing how we show up in life. In the face of extreme happiness or extreme tragedy, we still get to choose how we respond. It's important to remember that attitude and outlook come from our own inner choices – not what's going on around us.

Living intentionally also means deciding what we want and going for it. That means everything from a telephone conversation to your choice of career. The important thing is to choose the essence of what we want without getting attached to the end result. So if for example, I set an intention to be a powerful healer that could mean I could be a medical doctor or a teacher. It's the essence of healing which is most important.

In the short run it can mean setting an intention to show up for a meeting on time. Intentions apply to every aspect of life. The more intentions you set, the more intentional a life that you lead. And as the intentions are fulfilled to greater and lesser degrees our desires our refined.

As we refine our desires we open to an ever expanding life. And take my word for it – an expanded life is truly something to be grateful for."

Anne-Marie led the group through an exercise in setting intentions about what they wanted to get out the training they were embarking on.

"Our path on Earth is one of purpose and fulfillment. Here we learn the tools to pursue that path. However, many people are confused about what it means to be fulfilled.

I talk to people all the time who want more fulfillment in life. They think they can get it by doing something or waiting for something or hoping something will happen. Then they'll be fulfilled. I used to be like that – waiting for the day when happiness and fulfillment would come my way. There I was in a job I didn't much like. Talking about how I would find a way to do work with more meaning in the world. But you know that's all I was doing - talking about it. When I get more time, when I find a place to volunteer close to home, when I find a worthy organization that helps kids. That's when I'll join. That's when I'll make a difference.

Then I just stopped. I stopped waiting. I just lived. Stopped in my tracks and surveyed my own landscape. I looked at exactly where I stood in that moment. In that moment, I felt the difference. I finally got it. That's all there is – feeling. I know that I can choose to feel good no matter what's going on around me. It's not about what I do or even about my results.

Then I started listening. Listening to my heart. Now, for me, it's become all about how I do what I do. Do I do it fully? Do I give my all? Do I do what I do in joy and service? When I am doing that I'm not worried about fulfillment. I'm experiencing it. Being happy is really how we are, with people, on the job, in the circumstance.

Mostly it's about how we are with ourselves. That's where happiness and fulfillment lie. In giving what we have fully and with joy in every moment, no matter what we're doing.

By the way, the week after I "stopped", the perfect volunteer job appeared. Next I had a chance to move into a new position. Now I'm happier than ever.

We also practice the habit of passing knowledge and inner wealth from one generation to another. It's like the picture depicted in stained glass in the front door. The window shows an older woman passing the cup of knowledge to a younger woman. We must feed and support each other, our society – our world has gotten to this point in our evolution – socially, economically, physically by passing on the knowledge of past generations. Then we expand on it. We feed each other.

Bri felt a bit dazed as she wandered out of the room at the end of the day. Sarah was waiting for her in the hall.

"Wow, that was some first day, wasn't it?" asked Bri. "I wish Anne-Marie was going to be doing more of our training. "

Bri paused and looked around. It seemed as if everyone was both in a state of awe. All seven women stood in the hall chatting about the day.

"Me too, I've always known Anne-Marie had a presence about her. But today, it was as if she let so much more of her true Self shine through. She obviously has a lot of power and strength. Mom always said that about her but

I just didn't get it. I guess it would be intimidating if she showed her true power all the time," said Sarah.

Just then, Jessie turned to Bri and Sarah. She had obviously overheard them talking.

"I'll be so glad when I learn the tricks so I can turn it on like that. There are a few people I'd like to intimidate." Jessie smiled wryly.

"I really don't think that its a trick Jessie, I think Anne-Marie is a woman who knows who she is and understands her inherent power," replied Bri.

"Knowing all the Inanna secrets sure can't hurt," replied Jessie.

Bri shrugged as Jessie and her friend Debra strolled away slowly. "It doesn't seem like Jessie gets it. She thinks the power of the Daughters is in tricks," said Sarah huffily.

"Obviously, she hasn't known a lot of women who were genuinely empowered," said Bri.

CHAPTER NINE

The next day training began in earnest. Oya lead the class. She had been a daughter for nearly 40 years.

Oya spent the entire morning introducing them to the mirror and mirror training.

"The mirror is our most precious tool. We will have mirror training and practice every day. We start by seeing ourselves. Next we move on to more sophisticated uses." Oya looked around the room and smiled at the women.

"We use the mirror to strip away the doubt. We use the mirror to strip away the layers of falseness and uncertainty we have learned to carry. In the mirror we use there is no need for the trappings of the world. In our mirrors, God is always present. God is present in each of our young women, just as God is present in each human being.

In our mirrors the complications are removed. There are no insecurities in the mirror. No limiting beliefs. There are no other people's opinions in the mirror. When a Daughter is able to use the mirror without her personal lenses then the mirror reflects the best of what is and what can be. Only the truth of her soul remains.

"When a young woman sees the truth of her soul – clearly and unencumbered, miracles begin to happen. Some young women immediately get in touch with their soul's purpose and mission. Others become incredibly clear on a situation or a relationship in their lives. Still others find the courage to follow the dream that has always been present in them at some level of their being.

"In short, whatever will most propel the young woman forward is what she is able to see. She sees it by looking in her own eyes. She sees the possibilities.

"From that moment on the world no longer looks the same. Most women immediately assume complete responsibility for their lives. They see the potential in themselves and use that knowledge to launch themselves more fully into their lives and into the world. They step out of an ordinary existence into the truth of their own Divinity.

"Many of the women, you see today who are making a difference in the world, have been helped by the mirror.

"You see, once a woman sees the truth about herself, she can also see beyond herself. She sees the places in the world where she can help others. She sees the potential of the world where love, hope and compassion are reflected. She finds the cause bigger than herself that can change the world."

Oya paused.

"It takes some women years to become proficient in using the mirror. So be patient with yourself and with each other. Now everyone, take your hand mirrors and gaze into your own eyes," instructed Oya. She walked around the room, dimmed the lights. She also lit candles and incense.

"Ask silently for the Goddess to show you what you need to see."

At first no one saw anything but her own reflection in the mirror. Oya walked to the room offering advice and encouragement to the women. She ran them through short exercises in using their eyes and training their minds. Just when they were about to finish for the day, Bri looked into the mirror and saw an image of her mother. She looked very much like the photos Diana had shown her. As Bri watched, her mother turned and smiled. Tears streamed down Bri's face.

"Are you all right, Bri?" asked Oya.

"Yes, Yes, I just saw my mother and she seemed to smile at me."

"My, my, that's wonderful. You're a natural. Are you sure you haven't done this before?"

Bri shook her head no and wiped her eyes.

"Did anyone else see anything at all?" asked Oya.

"Just my own eyes and I don't think Bri really saw anything either." Jessie muttered to Debra. Sarah glared at Jessie and started to speak. But Bri put her hand on Sarah's arm to stop her. "Just let it go."

"But, I thought you said we'd start by looking at ourselves in the mirror. How could Bri possibly see her mother?" asked Kathy.

"Some images and ideas, like love can't be contained. They're always present. When we open our hearts sincerely, sometimes they find the space to come through," replied Oya.

"All right then, class dismissed. Remember, we have much more instruction before you can attempt to see the images on your own. The untrained often see what they fear or what they desire instead of what is. We wouldn't want you to act on false information." Oya stood by the door as the women ushered out one by one.

"That was very good, Bri, just like your mother." Oya said quietly as Bri left the room.

CHAPTER TEN

The old converted ballroom served as a common room in the house. It was certainly the most modern room in the house.

The furnishings made it a great room to study or hang out in. There were two large comfortably overstuffed couches, two large library tables to spread out on and a grouping of chairs to settle into for conversation. Some of the women in the house gathered there often for companionship. It gave them a place to study, commune and to compare notes. Sarah and Bri hadn't spent much time there during their first month of their training.

"Wow, it's been a crazy month. I can't believe all that we've learned. I don't know if I'll ever understand all the constellations and star charts." Bri closed her notebook and put her head down on top of her hands.

"All you really need is a methodical plan for studying. I've got it all worked out here. I can help you if you like. But you'll have to put in the time." Kathy turned and smiled at Bri.

"Thanks Kathy, but I'm not up to it right now. What I

could really use is some ice cream. I checked the freezer earlier, no luck. Anyone up for a late night run for comfort food?" Bri looked around the common room to see if there were any takers. She was not surprised to see only Kathy, Dana and Sarah.

"I'm game," answered Sarah, closing her book.

"But it's ten minutes to eleven, you'll never make it back before curfew," warned Kathy.

"Curfew, smurfew, when a woman needs ice cream nothing will stand in the way," answered Sarah.

Dana looked over, giving them a worried look. She seemed to be about to speak, but Kathy spoke first.

"Don't blame me if you get caught," said Kathy as she gathered up her books. "I'm off to bed, you should go too. Mother will have your head if you fall asleep in class."

"You go ahead to bed, Kathy. We're on a mission." Bri and Sarah headed towards the back door.

Bri and Sarah met on the landing between the second and third floors on Sunday morning.

"I know it's only been a month, but it feels like we've been studying this stuff for years. I am so glad we have Sundays off. It's really good of you to invite me to brunch with you and Helen. Are you really good friends?" asked Bri.

"Mom used to come to the house for meetings and leave me in the kitchen with Helen. She's like family to me. Helen used to sneak me goodies my mother never let me have. It helped to have Helen to talk to when my Mom was in one of her secret meetings," answered Sarah.

The two women headed down the stairs towards the kitchen. When they were near the bottom of the stairs they met Jessie on her way up. She had obviously heard part of their conversation.

"I don't believe the way you two hang out in the kitchen with that Helen woman," said Jessie. "She's a disgrace to the Daughters you know."

"Helen is an honest, caring and loving woman. But I can see how you wouldn't relate to that. I really don't care what you consider to be a disgrace, Helen is my friend." Sarah stormed off towards the kitchen and Bri followed.

"Wait a minute, Sarah," Bri stopped the other woman when they were around the corner and away from Jessie. "What was that all about?"

"Jessie's a snob. She thinks that just because Helen didn't go on to apprenticeship with her class, that she's not as good as the rest of us. Humph. Helen's heart would fill a coliseum. Jessie's wouldn't even fill a thimble."

"I agree. I would trust Helen with my life. But why didn't she finish with her class?"

"I don't know if anyone, except maybe Anne-Marie and Diana know. Mom certainly doesn't. She loves Helen like a sister. Whatever happened obviously didn't destroy Helen and Diana's relationship. Helen takes care of us like we're her children. Jessie is just...well I'm trying not to use that kind of language anymore. Besides if there had been some horrible scandal she wouldn't have been allowed to stay at Windmere House."

"I'm sure you're right. But I do wonder what happened. Let's go, Helen's waiting for us, so we can go to brunch."

As they were approaching the kitchen, Bri wasn't sure why, but she put her hand on Sarah's arm to stop her from entering immediately.

"I still don't understand why she was invited to join. Her mother was one of those involved in the mutiny," they heard Helen say.

"We don't punish the children for their parents' errors," replied Diana. "Jessie has shown some promise as a potential daughter."

"She's shown promise as a spoiled, self-centered brat if you ask me."

"We're hoping that she finds her true Self in the training. The discipline and encouragement has brought out the best in a lot of women."

"I don't know, Diana. I just don't trust her."

"I appreciate your concern, Helen. You have a great day. I'm off to meet a friend."

Bri and Sarah waited a moment. They heard the back door open and shut. Then they entered the kitchen.

"Oh there you are. Are you ready to go then?" asked Helen.

"I'm as hungry as a horse," replied Sarah.

"Just let me get my jacket. I'll be right back." Helen walked back to get her things.

"There you go," whispered Sarah. "I knew that Jessie was a bad seed. Helen can see it.   She's always been an excellent judge of people."

"I don't understand why Diana and Anne-Marie can't see it.   Jessie has no respect for the Daughters or our heritage," replied Bri.

Bri and Sarah heard humming outside the door. They knew that meant Helen was returning.

"Shall we go?" asked Helen.

CHAPTER ELEVEN

On Monday morning the women filed into the family room with their yoga mats and blankets.

"From now on, the first hour of every morning will be spent in silence," said Mother.

"Are we going to learn specific meditation techniques?" asked Kathy.

"Not until much later," replied Mother. "First we must learn to be silent with our own thoughts. Then when you are disciplined to that, we will teach you how to go beyond your own thoughts into the void.

Silence is more precious than gold. Silence is where the birth of all new ideas takes place. They begin in the void and move into the mind.

However, most minds are so active they can't begin to let the wisdom of the void through.

That's why it's important that we first learn to be with ourselves. Listen to your thoughts and let them go. For most of you this will be the beginning of a time when you come to know exactly what motivates you, and what holds you back. You will discover your inner voices: the inner critic and the voice of truth. Listen to them both. Learn to recognize the difference between the two.

Don't hold onto what is said. You will become accustomed to hearing them. Later we will begin teaching positive self-talk. You will be able to use this to replace the inner critic. During other times of the day you can feed your mind messages of truth and confidence. When you are able to silence the inner critic, the voice of truth will preside. But until you learn to listen to both voices, you cannot choose. So our hour of silence begins today."

Mother walked to the center of the room. "Find yourself a comfortable spot on the floor. Use your pillows and mats. Remember I'll be watching for any of you who doze off during this time."

A few days later Bri and Sarah were once again sneaking in after curfew.

"Shhh, it's almost midnight. We don't want to be caught coming in after curfew." Sarah tried to turn her key in the lock as quietly as possible. "Hmmm, that's strange it doesn't seem to be locked. This door is always locked."

"Maybe Aimee forgot to lock it when she came back from the gym." Bri followed Sarah in through the back door to the kitchen. "Whatever. I'm locking it now though. Don't turn on the light. The light in the refrigerator will be all I need. I'm just going to get some juice before I go up."

Both women continued to whisper so they wouldn't disturb Helen, whose room was right next door.

Bri got her juice and sat down at the kitchen table. Sarah leaned on the counter as they talked.

"I've always had a thing about the full moon. There's just something about seeing it reflect off the bay that makes me peaceful. If I could only get my mind to be that quiet during our hour of silence in the morning, I'd be doing well."

"Thanks for taking me with you, Bri. I never knew about that spot. It's a great place just to sit and relax at night."

"I was glad to have you. Sometimes when I'm there really late, I just stay in the car. You know to be safe. But I felt safe knowing there were two of us. Well, it's getting late let's go up."

Just as they reached the door to the rest of the house, they heard a sound.

"Shh, what's that?"

"Well, I'm pretty sure it's not Kathy trying to sneak in after curfew." Bri joked.

"I don't know if she could break a rule if she tried." Bri walked back to the door and Sarah followed.

Bri got to the back door just in time to see someone turn and walk quickly away. It looked like a woman, looking furtively over her shoulder.

"Did you see that?" asked Bri.

"You don't think someone left the door open to let him in do you? Maybe Debra's got a boyfriend she's trying to sneak in."

"That'd be way too risky. The walls are way too thin. Besides, it looked like a woman to me."

CHAPTER TWELVE

Bri walked past Jessie's room on the way to breakfast the next morning. She paused outside the door when she heard the conversation.

"Well, I did my best. The door was unlocked." Jessie paused. "Yes, I'm positive. I checked it twice before I went up. Yeah, that was at 11:45. There wasn't anyone around. Not even that troublesome Helen." Jessie stopped speaking again. "Well, whoever you think you saw wasn't around when I went up. We'll just have to create a new plan for you to find them. Look, I've got to go. Can we talk about this later? I'll come by around 7 tonight."

Bri realized that was all she would hear and hurried down to breakfast.

It wasn't until the lunch break, that Bri had a chance to tell Sarah what she'd heard. They went out onto the front porch and sat on the steps.

"So what do you think it means?" asked Bri.

"I have no idea. Who could Jessie have been trying to let into the house? Surely if it was guy, she would have been there to meet him. And you said she was talking about finding something. "

"Yeah, it must have been someone who already knows their way around."

"Do you think we should tell Diana?"

"No, we don't know what it was all about. Maybe it was innocent. Besides we don't want to let on that we were out past curfew. She's out of town again anyway."

"Hmm, Jessie and innocent just don't belong in the same sentence. But you're right, no point in being snitches. Looks like it's time to go back." Sarah got up and went back into the house. Bri waited a moment, thinking, and then she followed.

That evening, Bri woke up in the middle of the night. Instead of trying to go back to sleep, she decided to go down to the library in search of some of her family history. However, once she reached the library she was drawn to the corner where an old fashioned silver framed mirror stood.

Bri looked into the full-length oval mirror. At first she saw only herself. Slowly the image before her began to change. The mirror was filling with dark gray angry clouds. These were quite different than the white fluffy clouds Bri had seen in the mirror before.

Out of the clouds an image began to emerge. It was the image of a woman. The woman was clearly confident, late fifties and successful. Dressed in a tailored red suit, her accessories were perfectly matched to her outfit. She looked to be the image of success. As Bri watched, the woman suddenly became enraged. She was having an argument with someone. The cool veneer she had exhibited a moment ago quickly dissolved into a fit of rage. Another woman slowly appeared in the mirror. When Bri could finally make out the face she was shocked to see that it was Jessie.

In the space between the two women, just above their heads, a new cloud appeared. This one was glistening, glistening as if with a heavenly light. On the cloud appeared something Bri had never seen before, but instantly recognized. It was a very old, enormous, ornamental book. On the heavy wood cover was a carving of the Goddess Inanna. It was the sacred book, "The Goddess Documents." Sarah had told her she suspected it existed.

As Bri struggled to make sense of what she was seeing the image faded. Bri stood there for a while longer but nothing else appeared in the mirror.

"No, we can't go to Diana now. We don't really have any proof do we?" Sarah said after Bri finished her story the next morning. Sarah was adamant that they needed to keep investigating before turning to Diana for help.

"Besides you'll get in horrible trouble," continued Sarah.

"So what if I used the mirror? Well, O.K. I know we haven't been fully trained with the mirrors yet. But what am I supposed to do? Pretend I don't have the sight?" Bri complained.

"You never told me, why were you in the library last night at all?"

"It was strange. I was sleeping and then I woke up, quite naturally, as if I had slept through the night. But when I looked at the clock, I saw it was 2 am. I felt so rested that I decide to go down and have another look at the pictures of my mother that Diana showed me before. But when I got to the library, before I turned on the light I saw a soft glowing light coming from the mirror. So I walked over to it to investigate."

"And that's it?" asked Sarah.

"Yes, what did you expect, a voice that guided me down there?"

"Well, it may not have been a voice, but you were certainly guided there."

CHAPTER THIRTEEN

"Hope can come from the most unexpected sources," Mother began.

"Let's look at a case study of a woman we'll call Eve. She was being physically abused by her husband. At the time we became involved, Eve had a four-year-old little boy, a job as a receptionist at a used car a lot and a husband that beat her up. She was ashamed to talk to any of her friends about her situation. Her husband's drinking was getting progressively worse and Eve's self-esteem was at an all time low. She had no family to turn to. Eve was afraid that if she left her husband, Doug, he would hurt her or their son Aaron. However, Eve knew that if she stayed with Doug, Aaron was bound to pick up some of his behaviors. Eve had also become terrified that if Doug kept getting worse he would turn his rage towards their young son.

"This is where the Daughters entered. One of our Counsel members was alerted to the situation. All cases come through Windmere House for assignment to an available Daughter. In this case that was Linda.

"For this type of case we usually like to combine personal intervention with mirror intervention.

"The Daughter assigned to the case first did some investigation to find out where to make her entrance into Eve's life. In this case, the Daughter looked first at Eve's work situation. At the used car dealership where she worked, there were several possibilities. She could enter as a parts supplier, repair shop personnel or even as a sales person. Our Daughter found her way in by accepting a job as a salesperson in the lot.

"From that point, our Daughter began to work to develop a relationship with Eve. Soon the two were having lunch together. Linda knew that Eve wasn't likely to open up about her situation. So our Daughter talked about a friend of hers who had been in a similar situation until very recently. Eve wasn't suspicious because in her mind there was no way that Linda could have known what was happening in her home. Linda casually mentioned another friend who counseled women locally.

"At the same time Linda was able to see Eve's genuine talents and abilities up close. She subtlety encouraged Eve to have confidence in her ability to relate to people. Eve had proved that skill over and over again in her position as receptionist. Linda also found out that Eve had practically grown up in her father's used car lot. She had learned just about everything about the business.

"While all of this was going on during the day, we used our mirrors to help Eve through her dreams. In her dreams, Eve was able to envision several scenarios where she could leave her husband, Doug once and for all. She also saw a new career for herself using her talents to sell used cars. She realized that the additional money she could make would give her independence from her husband Doug.

Now, realize – Eve didn't remember all of the dreams that she had. She only remembered bits and pieces. But the seeds were planted that bolstered her confidence.

"Soon, Eve found the courage to leave Doug. She got the name of a counselor, found a safe house and moved herself and her son out of that situation.

"That was three years ago. Now Eve is on her own with her son Aaron. They've moved to a new state and the divorce is final. The ex-husband has moved on and doesn't have the time, money or the interest to pursue Eve or a relationship with Aaron. Aaron is developing into a strong intelligent young man who respects women."

"And they all lived happily ever after", whispered Jessie.

Debra just smirked.

"But I don't understand how we use the mirrors to enter women's dreams", said Aimee.

"That, my child is much too advanced. You'll learn all about that when you apprentice with a practicing Daughter," replied Oya.

Bri and Sarah were the last two women to leave when that session was over.

"Wow," said Sarah. "Sometimes, I can't believe I'm finally here. I've been looking forward to this training for so long it still seems unreal.

I've always dreamed of touching someone's life. Of really helping them."

Bri smiled back at Sarah, "Yeah I know what you mean. I guess that's why I became a lawyer. Only it didn't work out like I expected.

"I'm amazed at all that goes into just setting up an assignment. All the pieces had to fit perfectly for the Daughter to have been able to help that woman, Eve. That's a lot of research and work." Bri picked up her things as they prepared to leave the makeshift classroom.

"I knew there was a lot of research involved. Mom would sometimes spend weeks setting things up. She would call it her research projects. I think that was one of the reasons she was so happy I worked in insurance claims. She knew I'd get some background in investigation."

"Well, at least you're prepared. It makes me wonder how I'll be able to handle it all. I never practiced the type of law that involved that kind of legwork."

"That's one of the reasons we apprentice for two years. It gives us a chance to work closely with two or three experienced women. We see how they do it. Plus, there's a research specialist we can work with. She works out of New York, I think. I hear she's amazing, not only at the research, but also at coming up with creative ways to reach the girls and young women. She's been at it for 30 years or so, I think. Mom says she's incredible."

CHAPTER FOURTEEN

"Today, we're going to be doing some exercises on finding your purpose." Mother breezed into the room.

"But if we're going to be Daughters why do we need to find our purpose? I thought our purpose was helping young women achieve their dreams?" asked Aimee.

"Yes, that's one of the missions of the Daughters. But each one of you needs to clarify for yourself why and how you want to do this. Not all women in the lineage are invited to be Daughters. Not all women who are invited accept. Not all of the Trainees go on to apprenticeship. Why are you here?

"We don't want anyone to lose herself in becoming a Daughter. On the contrary, we want each Daughter to become more of who she really is.

"We each have individual strengths, passions and aptitudes. Discovering and developing those areas that are personal and unique to each of us is one way we keep our spark alive. It's also one of the things that keeps the Daughters vibrant through the centuries.

"Part of my purpose is teaching young women. I'm able to do much of that here in Windmere House. I'm also able to use that skill out on assignment. However, there are several other ways I fulfill my mission of teaching. For example, once a year, I go to South America and work with young girls there. That's one way I maintain my identity as a person, separate from the Daughters.

"Other women do it by holding regular jobs or having businesses where they fulfill different aspects of their individuality and live their purpose. That's why we have Daughters who are doctors, artists and business women.

"That's not to imply that your career is your purpose. A career is only one aspect of fulfilling a life purpose. A purpose shows up in every aspect of your life, not just in the career you choose. It infuses everything you do and everything you are.

"Don't worry about getting some grand vision of what your purpose or mission is," Mother continued. "I only use those words because they are part of our popular culture today. What I mean is: What do you want?

Your personal desires are really the key to your purpose. Desires are born in the eternal realm. Whatever gives your soul joy is your key to finding fulfillment and happiness. It's the way you know what service you are here to share. Your deepest desires are motivators for what you are here to give the world.

Mother looked around the room. "OK, let's begin with a guided meditation." Mother turned down the lights and began.

The guided meditation lasted about twenty minutes.

When it was complete, Mother brought them back.

"When you're ready, become aware of the sensations in your body. Become aware of your feet on the floor. Feel the surface that your back rests against. When you're ready, open your eyes." Mother paused.

"Now I want you to write down the following: Three things that you love doing. Three things that you really want. Three things that you do well. Three things that others say you do well. Now write down your three highest values. We'll use these to distill your life purpose. Don't worry. We're not trying to get it all today. We'll be working with this until graduation."

After dinner, Bri sat at her desk, reviewing the day. She was once again, surprised at the depth of the Daughters. Of all the questions she'd had before entering training this was the one she'd had no idea she might be able to answer through the training and guidance of the Daughters.

She now understood that her dissatisfaction with her life before revolved around that one question. What was her purpose? How would she go about fulfilling it?

Her life had been going so well on the surface. She had a great career as a lawyer. She had even had a sexy, intelligent, and successful boyfriend. But over the last year, she had become more and more dissatisfied. She had realized that her work didn't have any real meaning to her anymore.

She had friends from law school who were involved in non-profit work. She'd considered that, but that didn't seem to be the answer.

Bri had realized that she needed something that suited her. Today, in that guided meditation, she'd gotten a glimpse. A glimpse of why she was here. Not just in Windmere House, but a glimpse of why she was born.

For the first time in years, Bri felt a sense of hope and encouragement that she could contribute something meaningful to the world. And for the first time in just as long, Bri felt really happy.

Later that evening, Bri went down to the common room. She looked around and decided it wasn't just her. Everyone here seemed more content than before. Aimee seemed relaxed in a way, she hadn't seen before. Given the time of the day, it looked as if she had even skipped her daily workout. Normally, she was crazy with nervous energy, if she even thought she'd miss her workout. Now she just looked calm.

Kathy was sitting quietly. For once she wasn't studying. That seemed to be all she ever did, was study and follow the rules of house. Dana was curled up on a couch, relaxing under a homey looking afghan.

Bri looked across the room and Sarah smiled at her. Bri hadn't realized until this moment how happy she was to have Sarah to share moments like this with. She'd never had a friend like Sarah before. Finding Sarah was easily one of the greatest benefits of joining the Daughters.

Debra and Jessie weren't in the common room. So Bri couldn't reflect on how or if today's session had any effect on them. Bri was happy they weren't there. The room seemed so much more peaceful and relaxed without them.

Bri sighed deeply and walked across the room to join Sarah in the armchairs near the fireplace.

CHAPTER FIFTEEN

"You girls are sweet to help me clean up like this. The girl who normally comes to help with the cleaning called in sick this morning." Helen smiled at Bri and Sarah.

"We're happy to help. You know how we love our little talks," answered Sarah.

The women continued to chat as they finished up in the kitchen. But it was obvious that Helen's mind was not completely with them.

"What's wrong Helen, you seem distracted." Sarah finally asked.

"Oh it's nothing. I just found the back door unlocked again this morning."

"You're kidding? We found it unlocked a couple of weeks ago when we, umm, stepped out for a breath of air."

"Don't pretend with me. I know the two of you have a bad habit of breaking curfew. That's why I wasn't worried until now. I thought maybe it was just carelessness on your part. But last night, I know you were in bed when I checked the door. That's when I started to get worried."

"What are you worried about?" asked Bri. She had grown to love Helen over the last several weeks. She really enjoyed their talks. Helen had wisdom on all sorts of subjects. She also didn't worry too often. She'd seen too much.

"There have been some strange things going on around here lately. Doors unlocked. Things moved." Bri and Sarah looked at each other as Helen continued to speak. "I don't like it. Diana can be some naïve and trusting sometimes. Oh she's brilliant and a wonderful leader. But sometimes she's just too kind-hearted for her own good."

"What do you mean?" asked Sarah.

"Well, she won't hear a thing I have to say when I tell her there's something funny going on around here. She says it just you, Trainees, being careless."

"You don't believe that though, do you?"

"Not for a moment. It's too much like the last time."

"The last time?" asked Bri.

"Yes, the last time was about 15 years ago."

"The last time what?" Bri tried not to sound impatient.

"Oh dear, it's comes with the power. Periodically, people try to get their hands on the source of the Daughters of Inanna's powers, onto the very things that bind us together and make us strong."

"You mean 'The Goddess documents?' "

"Yes, but there's more to it than that."

"Aren't they well protected though?"

"Yes, but every so often we get a Daughter who's been corrupted somehow, someone who knows about the secrets and wants them for herself."

"What happened last time, Helen?" asked Sarah anxiously. "I remember Mom returning from Asia suddenly. I was in high school. Mom had only been gone about a week. Then she was home. She left an assignment unfinished. That was so unlike her. Of course she wouldn't tell me what was happening."

"Someone tried to sneak in and get the treasures. Whoever it was, was never caught. Since then, they've been moved and better protected."

"Moved? I always thought everything of value was kept in the Ceremony Room? Where is the Ceremony Room anyway? I can't believe we haven't stumbled across it since we've been here." Sarah turned to Helen for an answer.

"Stumble across it? Oh no, it's much too sacred for us to allow anyone to stumble across it. I shouldn't be telling you this. But I think somehow, you're supposed to know. Come to my room, where we can continue talking in private." Helen led the way from the kitchen to her room.

"In the library, there is a hidden entrance. It leads two places. All of the Daughters are initiated in the first place, the Ceremony Room. Only a chosen few even know of the other room. It is very small and even more sacred than the Ceremony Room. This room, we call it the Inanna's Room, houses the Book, "The Goddess Documents". The Book are watched over by an ancient protective statue of Inanna herself.

The documents are certainly valuable and powerful. But we hold a certain protection because of the power within the original statue of Inanna. It's said that the Inanna herself created the statue to preserve her power and protect her followers. Certainly we place it at the center of what it means to be a Daughter of Inanna. I mean the Daughters do- well you know what I mean," Helen, paused, stroking her throat.

"Anyway, if the statue and the Book were to fall into the wrong hands, I think that might be the end of the Daughters. I guess that's why the Triad created the amulet."

"I've never heard of an amulet," said Sarah.

"The amulet is something else all together," continued Helen. "It holds the blood of the Triad. They created the amulet with a binding ritual. The Daughters are bound together as sisters and partners by the amulet. Without it that inherent connection each of the Daughters feels might just fade away.

"With those three items, we have immeasurable power, which of course, we rarely use.

"Over the last thousand years, each Counsel member has contributed something to the altar. There are diamonds, rubies, emerald and gold jewels. Having something from each member of the Counsel during every generation renews the bonds of the current generations to the power of our ancestors.

"Once initiated, Daughters can spot each other without introduction. Everywhere around the world the blood of the Triad binds the Daughters.

"I know I shouldn't have told you all of that. It's something that not even all of the initiated Daughters know, just the Counsel and a few others. I only know because I'm here in the house all of the time. It would be impossible not to know things."

"Don't worry." said Bri and Sarah simultaneously.

"There's no way we would let information like that get out. It could do too much damage." said Sarah.

Just outside the room, Jessie, turned with a sly grin and walked away.

"Well, it seems like every time I turn around my Mom's got another little secret. She's hinted about the Book. But I didn't even have a clue about the amulet or the statue," Sarah said later when they were up in Bri's room. "So, that's got to be what Jessie's up to. Between what Helen told us and the conversation you overheard she must be trying to get the power of the Daughters by stealing the artifacts."

"Do you really think Jessie's so ambitious that she'd go after all that power on her own? She has to be working with that older woman I saw in the mirror. But who is she?" mused Bri.

CHAPTER SIXTEEN

"What do you want with the archive photos anyway?" Helen asked as she showed them how the library was arranged.

"Well, sometimes, I feel at a loss since I didn't know about the Daughters until recently. And Sarah says she wouldn't mind looking with me because there are bound to be some old pictures of her mother" explained Bri.

"Yeah, I need some ammunition for the next time she calls reminding me to work hard and learn all I can. Besides, she just loves to tease me with cryptic messages about her assignments. Another few months and she'll finally be able to tell me what the "assignments" she's always working on are all about. I want to see what it was like for her before." said Sarah.

Bri and Sarah had decided to solve the mystery themselves. They would find out who Jessie was working with. Then, they could figure out how to stop her. They planned to go through the archives for clues about who the woman in Bri's mirror vision had been.

They had talked about telling Helen their plan. In the end they had decided that Helen had enough on her plate already with all of Windmere House to manage. Besides, she was much too motherly to let them investigate unheeded.

The next few weeks passed quickly. It was now almost Christmas but Bri and Sarah hadn't found the mystery woman yet. They were beginning to get discouraged.

Eventually, afraid they might be running out of time, Bri and Sarah talked to Diana. Unfortunately, Diana had not taken them very seriously.

Bri felt disappointed. She didn't understand why Diana wouldn't listen to them. Diana absolutely forbid discussing any of their theories with Anne-Marie. Diana had gone on and on about how Jessie was harmless and no outsider could ever penetrate the protections of the Goddess.

"But with everything we know, including Helen's intuition, don't you think we should do something?" pleaded Bri.

"Yes, I know you have exceptional mirror sight, dear, but that does not mean that you've mastered it. More than likely you got some villain from a movie tied into your perception of Jessie as being up to no good. I know the two of you don't get along. Attachment to righteousness is a sure way to cloud the mirror sight. Now, why don't you two go and get a nice cup of tea from Helen." Diana had sounded almost patronizing.

There had been nothing left to say, so Bri and Sarah turned and left Diana's office. Sarah looked as furious and defeated as Bri felt. They talked about giving up on trying to find out what was going on. Surely that's what Kathy would recommend.

Besides, maybe Jessie wasn't really after the power after all. At least they hadn't given away that Helen had told them about Inanna's room. Bri didn't think it would have helped anyway.

But still they couldn't give up, so they had gone back to the archives.

"It doesn't seem like we'll ever find out who she is. We've spent hours and hours pouring over these archives. The rest of the house must think we're crazy spending our free time locked up in the library." Bri put here elbows on the desk and rested her head in her hands.

"I don't know what we are going to do. It looks like we need a plan B." Sarah closed the book she had been looking through and stretched out on the couch where she had been sitting.

"Maybe Diana's right. Maybe I imagined the woman. Maybe that whole incident with the mirror was just born out of my dislike and distrust of Jessie. Maybe this is all a wild goose chase."

"I don't think so. You should have seen yourself when you told me about your mirror experience. Besides, you are the most advanced at the mirror of any one in our group. Oya says she hasn't seen a natural like you in 30 years. I trust you. We just have to keep trying.

"But what do we do next? We've been through about every book here."

"Let's take a break from searching the archives. Let's not even think about it for the next few weeks. We'll deal with it when we come back from the Christmas break." said Sarah.

"I'm all for that."

Together Bri and Sarah put the books, albums and documents back in their places and left the library.

CHAPTER SEVENTEEN

Bri hung up the phone and turned to Sarah. "It's confirmed. The hip's broken. My step-mother, Jules will be laid up for quite some time."

"That's too bad. Send her my love. I've never met her, but the way you talk, I feel as if I know her."

"I don't know, Sarah, maybe I should go be with Jules while she goes through this. After all, she's pretty much the only mother I've ever known."

"Didn't you say your half brother James would be there? After all, he still lives at home, Bri."

"But he's only 22. Maybe he can't handle it, although he's always had more sense and sensitivity than most young men."

"Your Aunt Tracy will be there won't she? Haven't you told me how close she and her sister are? It's a broken hip. She's got the best care. What could you possibly do? What's this really about anyway?"

"Sarah, don't you understand? I don't feel like I really belong here. I just found out about the Daughters a few months ago. I'm normally so sensible. It's so unlike me to make this kind of decision. I've basically turned my back on everything I've ever known. In a way it even feels like I've turned my back on my father. I mean, if he had wanted this life for me, surely he would have told me more about my mother and her life with the Daughters?

"Oh Bri, but don't you see? He was afraid he'd lose you. In some ways he must have blamed the Daughters for your mother's accident. If it hadn't been for the Daughters she would never have been on that road.

"Besides," Sarah went on, "That's part of the point of being here at all. We are really learning to make choices based on what's right for each of us individually. Then we get to help others do the same. You can't stop something so important because of what your father might have thought. And you really don't even know for sure what that would be."

"Maybe, but still, I feel like I have so much more catching up to do," Bri shrugged.

"I can tell you, for sure, that you belong here. You have a natural sense of self. You have such compassion. And no one can beat you when it comes to using the mirror. You are a Daughter through and through. Believe me, I've met some women, children of my mother's friends, who don't have the sense God gave them. They would make horrible Daughters. Look, Anne-Marie and Diana have impeccable instincts. Being in the lineage doesn't guarantee you'll be invited to join. But you were. Doesn't that tell you something?"

"I suppose..."

"Tell me the truth, Bri? Does it feel like you belong here?"

"Oh yes, I feel more at home here than I've felt anywhere in my life."

"That settles it, then. You're staying."

CHAPTER EIGHTEEN

Look who's decided to socialize with the common people," said Jessie the next evening as Bri and Sarah entered the common room after dinner.

"Why aren't you two off to your secret business?" asked Debra. "Wanted to see how the other half lived?"

"We're just taking a break from our research. We decided it would serve the book we're writing better if we took a short break."

"What is that book about again?" asked Kathy.

"Oh we're keeping that quiet for now. Letting our ideas incubate. Besides, we change direction so often, it'll probably be something totally different when we finish." Bri answered.

"Do you want to help me with this puzzle?" asked Aimee.

"I'd think they'd want to be studying," said Kathy. "All that time you're spending on your writing, you should think about using some of it to prepare for Initiate Exams."

Bri decided to study, while Sarah turned to help Aimee with her puzzle.

Over the next couple of weeks Bri and Sarah learned how much they had been missing out on by not being part of the group in the common room. They gained a new appreciation for Aimee and Kathy as they got to know them better.

Aimee used to be a columnist at a Washington state newspaper. One evening she read them a piece she had written for her column.

"I remember growing up in our house. My mother was so much fun," Aimee began.

"Music was always playing in my parent's house. My mother loved it. Just about any type of music was fine with her. I guess that's why one of us kids was always taking some kind of music lesson.

"My mother's love of music spilled over into all aspects of her life. If you watch television, you might see scenes of parents riding in the car trying to reason (or shout) their teenager into turning down the radio. When I was a teenager riding in the car with my mom it was often me who said, "Mom, can we turn it down?"

"My family used to say I could sleep through anything. When my mother rose at 5:30 a.m., she would turn the stereo up loud enough so that she could hear it on the top floor of our split level house while she dressed for work. Yes, I learned to sleep through anything. I had to.

"Music was really a symptom, though. It was a symptom of my mother's love of life. She loved music. She loved to sing in choirs. She loved to dance. She loved to go to parties. She really loved having parties. I guess she loved parties so much, because she loved people so much.

"My mother was always in search of new friends. She would look for them everywhere. To my embarrassment, that often included standing in line at the grocery store. I can't remember how many times I was with my mother when she would notice an item in someone else's cart and would strike up a conversation. 'Oh, you have a cat? I have a cat. I just love animals. Don't you?'

"My mother's love of music created some wonderful bonding experiences for us. Throughout my teenage years, my mother and I held season tickets to the Paramount Arts Center. We saw every musical that toured through town.

"We continued to do sporadic outings until recently. I remember the last show we saw together. It was Oklahoma. That was before.

"Before, the music stopped in my parent's house. My mother is still alive. She's doing pretty well, considering. Considering she has Alzheimer's disease.

"She gets around pretty well. She forgets a lot more these days. She still remembers the family pretty well. But sometimes, she forgets that my older brother died five years ago.

"My mother has changed. It's most evident in the music. Or lack of it. Her hundreds of compact discs mostly gather dust these days. She rarely listens to them. To me, that is the biggest evidence of change in my mother.

"She still volunteers. She still wants to have friends around. She still loves her animals. But she has forgotten her music. She doesn't wake to music anymore. She doesn't seek out the concerts on PBS. She doesn't even sing in the choir anymore.

"When people who know us, ask how my mother is, I say she's doing fine. Then I think about the music." Aimee paused to wipe her eyes. The room was quiet for a moment.

"That's really poignant. I didn't know you were such an awesome writer," said Sarah.

"It so sad to see someone you love slip away like that. Were there Daughters around to help you get through the tough times?" asked Bri.

"No. My mother was never a Daughter. I think in her efforts to be different from her mother she turned away. That's why my grandmother was doubly happy to see me become a Trainee. I think she believes my mother would have been happy and maybe wouldn't have withdrawn from the world if she'd become a Daughter," replied Aimee.

CHAPTER NINETEEN

After only two and a half months with the other Trainees, Bri felt strange to be at home in her own condo once again.   They got the traditional break over the Christmas holidays. The other women had all scattered to spend the time with their family and friends. Bri was taking advantage of the opportunity to spend some time alone at home. But somehow the condo didn't feel much like home anymore. At first she wandered from room to room making sure everything was in order.

Bri was glad that she would have a chance to catch up with her old friends Wendy and Barbara. That would be fun. Christmas Day of course would be spent with her stepmother and brother.

After Christmas, however, she found herself spending most of her time wanting to get back to Windmere House.

Bri would have given anything to be allowed to visit Windmere House during the holidays. With all the Trainees gone she could look freely for clues about the mystery woman.   Apparently, that was just a fanciful thought, anyway. Windmere House would be filled with Daughters of Inanna.

Daughters came from all over every year to participate in the Winter Solstice Ceremony. Diana had explained that they were all still too green and uninitiated to participate this year.

Bri would have traded her condo to be there. She would have loved to participate in the power and ceremony of it all. But more than that, she could have gotten a look at the Ceremony Room to see if there was a way the sacred statue and amulet were hidden there somewhere.

"How were your holidays, Bri?" asked Sarah.

"Well, it was great to have the break. But I've got to tell you; I missed you. And the other women." Bri added hurriedly.

"I know what you mean. I couldn't help but think about you rattling around that big condo on your own. Did you catch up with your friends?"

"Yes, but it just wasn't the same. I guess I hadn't realized how much I'm growing and changing as a Trainee."

"I felt the same way. I got together with some people from work. Wow, I had absolutely nothing to say. They didn't even notice though. They just kept chattering about how unfair things are at work. The workload is still crazy I guess. They just don't seem to realize they have a choice about the work they do and how they live their lives. Thank God, I've always known I'd be a Daughter. Otherwise, I might have been just as miserable."

"I can relate to where they are. I was beginning to feel like I was losing myself before I came here. I don't know where I would be without you and the Daughters."

"Well, I'm certainly glad to have you in my life. You're a surprise I never expected when coming into training."

The two women looked at each other for a moment, and then entered the house.

CHAPTER TWENTY

"Sorry, we missed breakfast Helen. We went out for a walk this morning." Sarah picked up a bagel off the counter.

"It was just what I needed. With all the time we've spent in the library lately, and the holidays, I haven't been as active as I like. It felt good to get the blood pumping again." Bri picked up the newspaper and absently scanned through several pages.

"Bri, don't you want some toast or something?" Sarah passed a plate towards Bri.

Bri held out her hand to take the plate, but it slipped right through her fingers and crashed on to the floor.

"Hey, be careful. We need those dishes you know." Helen walked to the closet to retrieve the broom.

"Sarah, look! It's her. The woman in the mirror." Sarah hurried over to look at the picture in the newspaper.

"The caption says her name is Victoria Stewart. She's an executive with Lerner-Goode Publishing."

"Is that woman in the paper again? She always loved the limelight." Helen returned with the broom.

"You know her?" exclaimed Sarah.

"Of course she was with the Daughters. That was before...oh my."

"Before what?" asked Bri.

"You don't know?"

"Know what?"

"Victoria was driving the car when your mother was killed," Helen put a hand on Bri's shoulder.

"The accident was just awful. They were leaving the house after a ceremony. There was a drunk driver. Victoria couldn't do a thing. She was horribly injured too. Her face was a mess. She had to have several reconstructive surgeries."

"No wonder we didn't recognize her," said Bri.

"Reconstructive surgery. That's amazing," replied Sarah.

"Are you o.k.? This isn't bringing back unpleasant memories, is it?" Helen was watching Bri closely.

"No, I'm fine. It's just such a surprise. I never knew the details of the car accident that killed my mother. I was only told that she was leaving a friend's house. My stepmother just recently told me it was Windmere house. I had no idea there was anyone else with her."

"Bri, there's so much about your mother you don't know. We'll have to see what we can do about that," said Helen.

"There'll be time for that later." Bri took a deep breath. "Tell us more about Victoria. Why isn't she in any of the recent photos? There are pictures from just about every ceremony. Isn't she active in the Daughters anymore?"

"Victoria left the Daughters shortly after the accident. There was a huge disagreement. She felt she missed out on being elected to the Counsel because of her accident. But the truth is only a few voted for her. She enjoyed the power too much if you know what I mean. There was only one open spot. Sarah's mother was elected."

"Victoria was very upset, wasn't she? I remember my mom talking about going through a hard time right after she was elected," said Sarah.

"Yes, Victoria tried to stage a coup. She tried to split the Daughters apart. Some of those who had always admired Inanna's darker side were drawn to Victoria's case. They felt with her on the Counsel, they had a chance of using the power of Inanna for personal gain."

"Mom said the battle went on for nearly a year."

"Yes, that's when Victoria began her reconstructive surgeries. Without her focus, the dissenters fell apart. She tried to pull her supporters together after her surgeries, but it was too late. She hasn't been around here since."

"What do you mean about Inanna's darker side?" asked Bri.

"Well Dear, Anne-Marie likes to say that every light casts a shadow. Inanna's no different. In fact if you buy into some of the mythology surrounding her, Inanna is more shadow than light. Of course we know better. But wherever there is power, there is the opportunity to exploit it. Some people are drawn to that opportunity," replied Helen.

Later after leaving Helen, Bri and Sarah talked about what to do next. "Now we know who Jessie is working with. We know what they're after. We know it's potentially devastating for the Daughters. Do you think we should go back to Diana and blow the whistle on Jessie and Victoria?" asked Bri.

"No, I still don't think she'd listen. Besides, she'd know that Helen told us too much. Not only would we be no closer to stopping them, but we'd also get Helen in trouble. We have to find some way to stop them ourselves," answered Sarah.

CHAPTER TWENTY-ONE

"Today we'll talk about Mother Earth," began Oya. "As Daughters we have ceremonies around Earth's most sacred days. Most everyone knows about the winter and summer solstice. But there are others.

"We honor the earth as our home and school. We respect Earth as the mother of all life. We are merely expressions of Mother Earth. The wisdom of Earth can guide us in so many ways if we only let it.

"In our tradition we connect with Mother Earth through ritual, celebration and meditation.

"Although the goddesses exist on and beyond this Earth plane, our minds connect with the infinite through our bodies because we are uniquely a part of the Earth.

"From now on I want you all to spend an hour in nature every day. Listen to Mother Earth. Listen to her children, the trees, the wind and the rocks. Realize how important that connection is to our very nature as Spiritual Beings."

Bri and Sarah spent the evening discussing what to do about Jessie and Victoria.

"We'll just have to stop them ourselves." Bri said.

"I have an idea. Let's search the basement. The ceremony room was down there until about fifteen years ago. Mom was so excited when they created a special room for the ceremonies. But I still remember when I was little and dying for a chance to find out what Mom did in the basement. Maybe we'll find a clue down there. Or at least be inspired by the energy." Sarah had a far off look on her face.

"Well, when shall we do it?"

"How about tonight? We just need to wait a couple of hours until everyone's asleep. How about if I come to your room about one?"

"I'll see you at one."

At one o'clock sharp, Sarah knocked softly on Bri's door. She had two flashlights. She handed one to Bri and kept the other for herself.

Silently they went downstairs. In the kitchen, Bri slowly turned the old-fashioned crystal doorknob that led to the basement. Together, they crept slowly down the stairs.

"What's wrong?" asked Sarah. "You look like you've seen a ghost."

"Not a ghost, just a case of déjà vu." replied Bri. "This is all so familiar."

Sarah stopped.

"Now you look funny," said Bri. "But not like you've seen a ghost, more like the cat that swallowed the canary."

"Oh, it's nothing." Sarah grinned. "Just tell me what's so familiar about all this."

"Well, it's like I've done this before, sneaking down these stairs... Oh my God! It was you!"

"It's about time you remembered." Sarah laughed out loud.

"Shhh. We don't want to get caught. You knew all along?"

"Yeah, we should talk about it later."

Bri and Sarah split up and searched the basement. All remnants of the ceremony had been removed. It now looked like any other basement. Fifteen minutes later they were back up in Bri's room.

"So I was saying... You knew all along?" asked Bri.

"Well it took a while for the tumblers to click into place. But eventually, I figured out it was you. I remembered another little girl, but until recently I didn't have a name.

"I remember that night. I remember us sneaking down the stairs so clearly. Of course it helps that my mother told that story over and over to any one of the Daughters who would listen. I knew I should never have told her. But my six-year-old conscious couldn't hold onto all the guilt. I confirmed it was you by talking to Mom."

"But why didn't you say anything to me?" asked Bri.

"No point in bringing up something you don't remember. Unpleasant memories you know. Umm, that was right before your mother died."

"Yeah, well...that was years ago. " Bri seemed lost in thought for a moment. "So that's why it feels like we've known each other forever. We practically have."

All of a sudden memories of playing in Windmere house with Sarah came flooding back. Sarah and Bri spent a couple of hours reminiscing and checking each others memories for accuracy, laughing about their silly antics. The tears and the laughter came again and again for both of them.

"I feel like I've found a long lost sister," said Bri. It was now very early in the morning. Sarah and Bri held eye contact for a moment before Bri looked away.

CHAPTER TWENTY-TWO

"Last week you talked about the Earth." Diana began. "You talked a little about how our bodies relate to the Earth. Let's explore that a little more today. We've talked a lot about being spiritual beings living on a human plane. But what does that really mean? Does that mean that we should ignore the physical aspect? Why were we given bodies anyway? Who has some ideas?"

As usual Kathy's hand was the first one in the air.

"Yes Kathy?" asked Diana.

"Well, we were given bodies to navigate the planet, right?" Kathy seemed pleased with her answer.

"Yes," answered Diana. "Anyone else?"

"Well, I think we were given bodies to experience pleasure and pain." Jessie looked over at Debra and winked.

"Yes, that's a good answer too, but what about communication? Does anyone think that communication could be one of the primary reasons we have bodies while here on Earth?"

"Well, we talk and listen, with our bodies. And we communicate with touch, and looks. I guess we really use all of our senses to communicate," Aimee seemed to ponder her answer as she spoke.

"Absolutely, true! But let's take it one step further. What if, every day, all day long our bodies were giving us signals? What if our bodies understand what's happening in the world better than our conscious minds?" Diana paused. "Any thoughts?"

"You mean like when I'm about to do something I shouldn't and get that little feeling in the bottom of my stomach?" asked Bri.

"Or when I get that warm feeling inside when I hear the voice of someone I love?" asked Sarah.

"Very good!" answered Diana. "Every day in thousands of ways our bodies are sending us little signals. If we get really good at listening to them, we can even tell when someone is telling the truth or a lie. The body can't lie. So much of connection and human relationship goes way beyond the verbal. It goes way beyond touching one another. Our bodies are a bridge to that place where we are all connected. Once we, as a species, all get really good at listening to them, we'll need a lot less words." Diana paused and looked around the room before continuing.

"We don't have any mothers in the room, but I'm sure we can still all relate. What about the bond between a mother and her baby, the feeling that tugs at the heart? That's really what relationship is about. We just need to understand it more."

"But how do we practice?" asked Kathy.

"Fortunately, there are a number of ancient and modern techniques we can use. We can become aware and connected with our bodies through practices like yoga and Tai Chi. We can practice listening and communicating with our bodies with Gestalt techniques. We can also reach into the subconscious mind that is our body, by working with a very special technique. That's where we'll start out today."

"That was pretty cool stuff we did with the body today," Sarah told Bri later.

"I know I just started to realize how much I've ignored my body, recently, especially since I've started to do yoga. It's kind of like waking up to a new reality."

"Yeah, I've been doing yoga for years. But still, I never really thought to listen to my body when I had a big decision to make, or to decide if I should trust someone. Sometimes I would get a strong feeling, but overall, it just wasn't a consideration."

"My analytical brain really liked the research, Diana showed us. I would never have believed that scientists are proving that we can actually detect the truth through things like applied kinesiology. I'm definitely going to be doing more research into that stuff."

"You two are just wasting your time." Jessie sailed into the dining room. "I'll be using my body for more traditional pleasures this evening."

"Having dinner with your boyfriend again? Do you ever eat dinner here?" asked Bri.

"Not if I can help it. Michael takes me to the most wonderful places. A lot of times we just skip dinner and go straight to the body kinesiology, if you know what I mean."

"I don't know how you do it and make it back by curfew," Kathy chimed in.

"Come on Debra, Michael's bringing his friend Kenny." Jessie said as Debra walked into the room.

The two women left the room, with their heads huddled together. Just as they reached the door, their loud laughter drifted back into the room. Kathy shrugged as she left the room.

"I'm having a really hard time being in the same room with Jessie these days," complained Sarah.

"I know what you mean. Just knowing she's involved in a plot to hurt the Daughters makes me want to wring her neck," replied Bri.

"We'll get to the bottom of this. Then she'll get her due. I just hope it's soon enough," Sarah said half to herself.

CHAPTER TWENTY-THREE

"Perfection is really all there is in life. Everything we see everywhere is absolutely perfect. It's perfect because it exists. Anything we perceive as not perfect is only an illusion. Our minds play tricks on us. We think we know how things are supposed to be. But in reality we know so little. That's why we're here; to expand. We know we're getting it when what we see lines up in our consciousness as perfect. That is to say that when we realize perfection already exists; the tumblers click and the gates are opened. This happens piece by piece. That's the way we get it. When we're "there", then all that we see, we recognize as perfection. In the real world, that's all there is." Diane lectured. "Understanding that everything is always perfect leads us into gratitude.

"We have already spent a lot of time discussing and experiencing that what we focus on expands. What we are thankful for appreciates. In fact the word appreciate means to increase in value.

Gratitude is one of the most powerful forces in the universe. Gratitude springs from love and the recognition of perfection.

"But Diana, if everything is already perfect, then why do we do we help young women. Aren't their lives perfect already?" asked Dana.

"Of course they are. We just help them to see that. More importantly we help them see their own perfection. Once each of us recognizes another aspect of our perfection, then what we perceive in the world begins to line up with the real world of the Eternal," answered Diana.

Later in the day Bri and Sarah discussed their plans to catch Jessie and Victoria in the act.

"As secret as the council is about all of this, I'm sure that Jessie's never seen the original. We can surely create an adequate fake. We'll need to hunt around some antique shops for a very old looking pendant. We can create the statue ourselves out of clay." Bri seemed lost in thought.

"But how can we create a fake amulet and statue? There are way too many people around her for us to pull it off without anyone finding out." Sarah stared out the window.

Bri thought for a moment. "Well, we'll just have to use my Condo."

"But that would be breaking the rules. What would Kathy say?" Sarah looked at Bri for a moment. Then they both burst out laughing.

"There's still one major problem though. We can create these fakes. But what good does it do us if we don't know where the Inanna room is and how to get in.

"And what about the book?" asked Sarah.

"I've seen the book, at least in the mirror, Jessie hasn't. We can find something convincing at one of San Francisco's best used bookstores, I'm sure. We'll need to do something about the cover though. As for the room, I guess we'll worry about that when the time comes."

"I took a sculpting class in college," said Sarah. "So I think we can pull off the statue. We just need to look at some pictures ancient sculptures from the library. We'll probably need to make it, leave it at your place to dry and then go back to get it."

"Yeah, I used one of those faux aging processes on my dresser. I think that will work for the statue. We should probably get started right away though. We don't know how soon we'll need it," said Bri.

"I know how we'll be spending our next few Sundays. I guess we've just taken up antiquing. This might actually be fun."

CHAPTER TWENTY-FOUR

Bri woke up feeling both nervous and excited. She was looking forward to the day. She only hoped that she was up to it. It had been a long time since she'd been around kids.

Their new community service project started today. They had been doing a variety of community service work every month. So far they done neighborhood cleanups, worked at a homeless shelter and visited patients at the hospital.

But this project was different because it would continue through graduation. Beginning today, every Saturday, the Trainees would be working in a community youth center. Children from the ages of 7-18 attended the center. There were scheduled activities, homework help and field trips.

Bri figured if she wasn't any good at anything else, at least she could help with homework. She knew she could help kids with the English, History and Social Studies homework. Anything else might be a stretch.

Bri thought how interesting it was that now that she had finally pursued something just for herself was the time when she would become of most service. The way Bri looked at it, four days a month at the community center equaled at least as much service as what she had provided in a year in her career as a corporate lawyer. Bri almost laughed out loud when she thought about it that way.

Bri grabbed her bag and headed downstairs.

"Are you ready for this?" asked Sarah.

"I guess, I'm as ready as can be expected," replied Bri.

"You make it sound like you're going to a funeral or something."

"No, it just that I haven't really been around kids since... well since I was a kid."

"Oh you'll be great. I have two nephews. They're a ball. Just be prepared to stay on your toes."

"No problem."

Nine hours later, the seven women returned. They were all exhausted and ready to head upstairs for an early night.

Helen met them at the door with the news.

"There's been a break-in. We need all of you to check your rooms to make sure nothing is missing."

"What!" At least four women shouted simultaneously.

"Were you here, Helen? Are you o.k.?" asked Sarah.

"Oh, I'm fine.   I was at my sisters, like on most Saturdays.

"How did they get in?" asked Bri.

"What did they take?" asked Kathy.

"How about one at a time, o.k.?" replied Helen.

The seven women gathered around Helen as she explained what had happened. She'd come home to find the back door wide open.   Anne-Marie and Diana had been attending a women's luncheon. Neither Oya nor Mother lived in the house.

When Helen looked around, she saw that someone had been in the library. She said that nothing had been taken, but obviously someone had been looking for something. When Diana and Anne-Marie came home, they called the police, who came out and took a report.

"That's all there is to it. Nothing's missing, no one's been hurt. The police want us to verify that nothing is missing from your rooms." Helen turned and walked towards the kitchen.

The women stood in the hall speculating on what had happened. Then one by one they headed upstairs.

Bri and Sarah waited until everyone was upstairs and then headed for the kitchen.

"So is that it?" asked Bri.

"Did you tell all?" asked Sarah.

"Do you think it's related to the last time?" asked Bri.

"Is someone trying to get Inanna's power again?" asked Sarah.

"Are you done now?" asked Helen.

Bri and Sarah nodded their heads silently.

"Well no, I didn't tell everything back there. Someone got into the Ceremony Room. But luckily whoever it was didn't know how to get to Inanna's room. The fact that they got into the Ceremony Room almost guarantees it was a Daughter or former Daughter. That room is very well protected. Only insiders know their way in. Apparently they thought they could access Inanna's room from there. If they know about Inanna's room - and I suspect they do, they just don't know how to get to it."

"Oh my Helen, what did Diana and Anne-Marie say? Are they going to do anything? They didn't tell the police about Inanna's room, did they?" asked Bri.

"No, they just told them someone had been in the library. The police don't even know about the Ceremony Room. We couldn't let them dust for prints."

"What about Diana?" asked Sarah.

"She's in Anne-Marie's office. They called an emergency conference call for the Council." Helen looked at her watch. "It started fifteen minutes ago. Don't you worry; the Council will come up with something. They're the ones who had the Ceremony Room changed and Inanna's room put in place 15 years ago, after the last time."

"You must be exhausted, Helen. Why don't you go to your room and rest? We won't bother you anymore." said Sarah.

Helen nodded wearily and headed for her room.

Sarah and Bri decided to go for a ride so they could talk undisturbed. They were both pretty quiet until the car was parked by the ocean.

"I was watching Jessie while Helen was telling us about the break-in. She didn't seem too surprised." said Sarah.

"I know. If anything she seemed a little disappointed, that there didn't seem to be anything missing." replied Bri.

"Do you think she was involved?"

"Well. We know she was at the Center all day with us. But she could have tipped off Victoria that the house would be empty today."

"We better get to work. We want to have the fakes in place, just in case."

"I know there's no telling when they'll try again."

The women sat for a while staring silently at the ocean.

"Your dad must be great." Bri changed the subject. She had been thinking a lot about family lately. "He seems so supportive of you and your mother. He's not like some of the men that can't handle empowered women, is he? And the way your mom travels. He must be awesome."

"Yeah, my dad's pretty great. Sometimes, I take him for granted I think," replied Sarah.

"Well, tell me something about him."

"My dad demonstrates unconditional love in every way. He was always there for us. He's the kind of dad who was scout leader to my brothers. He's the kind of dad who chauffeured my girlfriends and me back and forth to the mall. He was at every school play and recital we ever had.

"My dad's a spiritual man by practical standards. He's always gone to church. But he's the rare man who could find a church in any community he lived in. He was never limited by the name that a church called itself.

"I've heard stories about how some men feel when they find out about the Daughters. Dad was only ever supportive."

"Wow, I thought people only had parents like that in the movies. You are so lucky, Sarah." Bri sighed.

"I know."

CHAPTER TWENTY-FIVE

"They're putting in an alarm. The Counsel hated to do it, but we're having an alarm installed. No one's to know about it except the Counsel and me." Helen filled Sarah and Bri in at brunch the next morning.

"Why do they hate the idea, so much?" asked Bri.

"It's the house." answered Sarah. They've done everything they could to protect the integrity of its late 19th century feeling. Except for the bathrooms and the kitchen, everything has stayed with that era. But why aren't they telling everyone about the alarms, Helen?"

"Well, the break-in yesterday, was obviously one of our own. No point in tipping off the culprit. I'm only telling the two of you because of who you are, and your heritage. With your mothers, there's no way you two could have gone bad. Besides, the way I've gotten to know you the past few months I'm sure it's o.k."

"We appreciate your trust, Helen. We would never violate it." Bri reached across the table and put her hand over Helen's.

"But if no one knows about the alarm what good is it? What about the alarm company? Are they going to be allowed into the sacred space? Doesn't it have to be set? What if one of us Trainees accidentally trips it," asked Sarah.

"Slow down, Sarah, of course the Counsel considered all of that. One of the Counsel Members is flying in tomorrow to install it. She's coming under the pretext of getting some information for an assignment. What she'll really be doing is installing the alarm. The alarm is going directly on the Ceremony Room and on Inanna's room. They'll be on the secret entrances. Unless someone's trying to get in, there's no way they can trip it."

"That's brilliant." Bri gave Sarah a worried look as Helen looked over at the buffet.

"I'll just go back for one more trip," said Helen, looking back towards the buffet.

"It's your day off. Enjoy yourself," replied Sarah.

CHAPTER TWENTY-SIX

The next few weeks seemed to pass very quickly. The Trainees kept up their pace on their studies and community service.

Bri and Sarah also kept busy putting together the pieces of their plan. They felt lucky that the alarm had been installed because it would buy them time to put their plan into action. Every so often they worried that Victoria and Jessie would try again before they were ready, but they continued with their plan.

"What's wrong Bri? You seem distracted," Sarah looked up from her studying.

"Did you see that girl I was working with at the community center?" asked Bri.

"Yes. You worked with her last week too."

"Her name is Sue. It seems like she's on the brink of becoming lost. She's not handling the transition to high school very well. She reminds me of myself at that time. If I hadn't had Ms. Day as a teacher, I'm not sure what would have happened. She really helped me find some direction."

"What's wrong with Sue? Is it just her self-confidence or something else?"

"Well, on the surface it's self-confidence. But my instincts tell me it's something more."

"So check it out."

"I've been thinking about it. It seems like such an intrusion."

"But you got something from her right? Something that's hers?"

"Just a pencil."

"That should be enough. Let's go to your room now. I'll meditate and hold the space, while you use your mirror sight." Sarah started gathering up her things.

Upstairs Bri got out the pencil she had gotten from Sue. She held it in her hands and sat at her desk. Sarah set up Bri's make up mirror on the desk. The door was closed. The candles were lit. Now Sarah sat on the floor, while Bri settled in at the desk.

Bri took a few cleansing breaths while Sarah started to meditate.

Bri rolled the pencil between her hands and stared into the mirror. She sat looking at her own image for a few minutes. Slowly the mirror began filling with grayish white clouds. It looked like a summer storm was rolling in.

Slowly, Sue began to appear in the mirror. She was standing by the lockers at school. Bri watched her laughing and smiling with what appeared to be a boyfriend. It looked as if Sue was making a joke. Suddenly the boy grabbed her by the wrist and jerked her forward. Sue looked terrified. A man in a suit came around the corner and the boy backed off.

Bri watched the mirror for a while longer, but the image had faded away. Bri turned and tapped Sarah lightly on the shoulder.

"Well?" asked Sarah.

"It's a boy."

"Isn't it always?"

"This is different. I think he's physically abusing her." Bri explained what she had seen in the mirror.

"That's awful," sighed Sarah.

"Yeah, but what do I do now?"

"Well, I'd say you have to go into her dreams."

"But I don't know how to do that. We've talked about it a little in class. But I wouldn't know where to begin."

"I've got an idea," said Sarah.

Once again, the women were back in the library. Sarah explained to Bri about a book of case studies she'd seen in the library.

"Mom didn't know I knew about it, but I used to sneak in here and read them. They were like fairy tales to me. Anyway, I'm sure that some of them have some pretty good detail in them. With what we know and what's in the book, I'm sure we can figure it out."

"How the heck are we going to find it? There are thousands of books in here."

"Just use your intuition. We'll find it. If I recall correctly, it's bound in dark green leather. It's not very thick, probably about a quarter of an inch."

The two women searched the library for a while in silence. Finally, Bri closed her eyes. She took a deep breath and spun around slowly in a circle. When she stopped she went directly to a shelf and put her hand out. She pulled out a small book with green leather binding.

"Is this it? It says *Case Studies of the Daughters of Inanna*."

"Damn, you're so good that sometimes you scare me woman," said Sarah who had been watching.

The library door opened. Kathy entered. Bri was so startled that she jumped. Quickly she put the book behind her back.

"What are you two doing in here? Didn't you spend enough time here last fall? What happened to that book you were writing anyway? Surely you're not starting up again, now? Not with Initiate Exams so close?" Kathy rattled on not waiting for a response.

"We're just getting a book to do some research. How about you?" Sarah asked.

"I'm just putting back this book on the history of the Daughters." She returned the book to the shelves and turned and walked out. Before leaving the room, Kathy stopped and looked back over her shoulder.

"By the way, I know you two are up to something. That's why I'm outta here. I don't want any part of it." Kathy left the room and closed the door behind her.

Bri and Sarah looked at each other, and then sat down with their heads together to study the book.

"Well it seems easy enough," said Sarah.

"That's easy for you to say. You're not the one that's going to be prying into someone's dreams," replied Bri.

"It's getting late. Let's sleep on it. If you feel o.k. about it, we'll do it tomorrow night."

The next night the two women sat together on the floor of Bri's room. It was after midnight. They had talked about it. Since they didn't know anything about Sue's home or what time she went to sleep, they figured the later the better.

They held hands as Sarah led a prayer. Bri set her intention to show Sue that which was for her highest good. After discussing it awhile, Sarah and Bri had decided to show Sue two scenarios. This case was almost identical to one of the case studies they'd looked at last night. In the first scenario, she continued down the path she was going with her current boyfriend. In the second scenario, she broke it off with the boy.

Bri and Sarah were curious. With dream work they didn't know how things would turn out. Once they got it started, possible outcomes came through from the Eternal.

When they were finished, both Bri and Sarah were surprised. They could pretty much have predicted that the first scenario of staying with the boyfriend would end up with the girl having very low self-esteem. But they hadn't known that she would end up barely graduating high school and going to work at a local convenience store.

In the second scenario, when Sue found her self-confidence, she broke it off with the boy, started volunteering with the younger kids at the community center, and entered a college program in early childhood education.

Bri and Sarah were able to watch all of this unfold as they gazed into the mirror they'd placed on the floor between them.

"Oh no, we've created another Kathy!" exclaimed Bri when the images had faded. Both women laughed.

"Seriously, just because we saw it in the mirror doesn't mean it will happen. It will still take some action by Sue. Then, it could still go in any number of directions. The early childhood education thing is just one possibility. It just shows Sue there is another way. She still has the free will to make whatever choices she wants." Sarah stood up and stretched.

"I know. Maybe there's something else I can do. I think I'll go by the center tomorrow before dinner. Sue might need someone to talk to." Bri's head was spinning.

The next evening after class, Bri ran into Jessie on the way out of the house.

"What's going on here?" asked Jessie. "Surely you're not going out on a date?"

"No, actually I'm on my way to the Community Center. I want to check on a young friend there."

"Friend? Don't you mean freak? Those kids there are the biggest bunch of losers I've ever seen. I will be so glad when I've served my sentence there, and here for that matter. When we finish Training, if I never see this house again, it will be too soon."

"Nobody's begging you to stick around here, you know. You can go whenever you please."

"Not a chance, we haven't even got to the good stuff yet. I wouldn't leave before I learned all the best stuff about manipulating people."

"You're unbelievable."

Bri was still fuming when she related the conversation to Sarah later that night.

"You know Bri, not everyone's good like you. There are people who actually follow the dark side Inanna," said Sarah.

"Well, I know that, but what about the dark side? We never talk about that in class. All of the history we've done on both Inanna and the Daughters – nothing about the dark side has been mentioned."

"The darkest interpretations of Inanna include a lot of ugly stuff. There is manipulation, promiscuity, a quest for power and some other really nasty things. We focus on the empowering aspects of Inanna here. Anyway, you know Jessie. Don't let her get to you. We're gonna stop her."

"Yeah, I know." Bri went to her room with a whole new side of things to ponder.

The next week when they returned to the Center for Volunteer day, Bri and Sarah were amazed at the changes in Sue. She was more outgoing and she laughed more. She was also getting more involved with the younger children's play. Later that day Bri overheard her asking Kathy what it was like to be a teacher.

Bri caught Sarah's eye across the room. Sarah just smiled and nodded.

CHAPTER TWENTY-SEVEN

"Well at least we don't have to worry about setting off the alarm when we sneak back in tonight." said Sarah.

It was close to 2:00 a.m. when Bri and Sarah returned to the house after working on the clay statue at Bri's condo.

"No, I'm more worried about falling asleep during silent time tomorrow. Last time I did that Oya took me into the hall and skewered me. Then she repeated a good portion of it at the end of the session, so the rest of you could hear." said Bri.

"I remember." Sarah smiled.

"It's not funny. Just because you've been meditating since you were nine. That's no reason for you to go all superior on me."

"No really, I was smiling because I was thinking about the look on Jessie and Victoria's face when they find out they pulled off a grand heist of worthlessness."

"Yeah, that'll be pretty good; I wish I could see their faces. Better yet, I wish the police could and they could be locked up for years."

"Yeah, but unless we know when they're going to pull it off, I don't see how we can get the police involved without telling them more than the Daughters want them to know."

"I know. Maybe they won't even get in. Not with the new alarm system and all."

"I don't know. A woman like Victoria has got to have some pretty sophisticated resources. If she finds out there's an alarm, I'm sure she can find her way around it."

"Speaking of getting around the alarm, what the heck are we going to do? How are we going to put the fakes in place?"

"I've been thinking about that. Maybe my mom will help. She's way more practical than Diana and Anne-Marie. I'll just have to figure out how to approach it. I'm sure she'll trust me now that I'm in Training."

"That'd be awesome. I'll keep my fingers crossed." Bri crossed her fingers.

Bri and Sarah caught up with each other later in the day.

"Did you talk to your mother?" asked Bri.

"Yes," said Sarah.

"And?"

"She wants to find out more. Of course she knows about the break in because she's on the Counsel. She wants to find out more about Victoria."

"I guess that's to be expected. I mean the only thing we have tying Victoria in is my mirror vision. How's your mom supposed to trust that? She knows I'm brand new.

She's never even met me." Bri sighed heavily, as she got her yoga mat prepared to go downstairs for their daily hour of silence.

"Hey, don't give up. If Mom weren't going to help us, she'd have said so straight out. The fact that she's going to do some more research is a good sign. She's looking for Victoria's motive. One of Dad's friends is pretty high up in the publishing arena. She's going to check with him to see if there seems to be anything funny going on. Plus, she's going to get the research specialist in New York checking to see if there's any other scuttlebutt."

"That's great. But how long is all of that going to take?"

"Don't you know? When the Daughters are on it, mountains move. It shouldn't be more than a few days, a week at the most."

"Let's hope that's quick enough."

The two women hurried off to class.

Bri and Sarah were on pins and needles for next couple of days. They spent half their free time running back and forth to the kitchen asking Helen if there was anything new from the Counsel.

"I really think we should set up surveillance on Jessie. You know stake out her room." Sarah looked over her shoulder to make sure no one else was coming out onto the porch.

"Yeah, that wouldn't give us away would it," Bri replied sarcastically.

"This waiting is just driving me nuts. I hope Mom calls me soon."

"It's only been three days, Sarah, give her time."

The next evening Sarah and Bri were again sitting on the front porch. They were sitting silently watching the traffic go by when Sarah's cell phone rang.

Sarah pulled it hurriedly out of her pocket. She looked at the display. Sarah answered mouthing "It's Mom."

All of a sudden Bri was nervous. She stood up and started pacing across the porch. The call seemed to go on forever. Bri eventually left the porch and ended up pacing across the lawn.

Finally Sarah hung up.

"Come on, let's go for a walk."

Once they were down the block a bit Sarah began. "Mom said that there's a lot of buzz at Lerner-Goode about a big deal coming soon. They're saying they are going to have the edge on all the publishing houses out there. There isn't any specific information except that it's something really big. Mom also says that up until last fall Victoria's job at Lerner-Goode was on the line. The board wasn't at all happy with how she was performing. That has all seemed to fade away in recent months, but no one's sure why,"

"Wow, your mom is good. Where did she get all that info?" asked Bri.

"Dad's friends in publishing, I guess. The good news is that based on everything she's heard, Mom's definitely willing to help us. First off she told us how to get to both the Ceremony room and to Inanna's room. Both of them are accessed through the library."

"That explains the break in, then."

Bri and Sara continue to walk as Sarah filled in more details from her conversation with her mother.

CHAPTER TWENTY-EIGHT

The next Friday night, Bri slipped into Sarah's room. Quietly she sat on her bed. Watching Sarah sleep for a moment, Bri couldn't believe the emotion suddenly pouring from her. She pulled herself together quickly and touched Sarah on her shoulder to wake her up. Sarah stirred. Bri whispered her name.

Sarah woke up suddenly, sitting up in bed.

"What is it?" she asked. "Has something happened?"

"No, everything is fine. I just realized that it will be tomorrow. They'll try to get into Inanna's room tomorrow." said Bri.

"How do you know?" asked Sarah.

"I woke a few minutes ago, and just knew. Then I started to think about it. Exams are finished. Tomorrow's our last Volunteer day before graduation. Diana and Anne-Marie will be at the restaurant planning our banquet. And Helen's never here on Saturdays. Diana and Anne-Marie probably think everything is safe since the alarm's been installed."

"It may well be. There's no indication that Jessie or Victoria know about the alarm."

"I know that. But like I said, I just know. Alarm or no alarm, we need to be here when it happens. Get up."

"What?"

"Get up." Bri got up off Sarah's bed.

"We need to take one of our cars and park it near the community center. Then we can sneak out after we get there tomorrow and come back here. We'll have to tell the counselors there that we're gone. But no one else needs to know. We'll ride over with everyone else and then sneak back here and catch the culprits."

"That's a great idea. Have you been thinking about this for awhile?" asked Sarah.

"Nope, it just came to me when I woke up."

"Your Knowing is good, girlfriend, really, really good. You're going to make a great Daughter."

"Yeah, that is if I don't get kicked out for what we're planning tomorrow."

Bri and Sarah snuck quietly out of the house. They dropped off one car and drove back to the house in the other. Then they quietly got their fake amulet, book and statue out of the car.

When they got back to Windmere house they went straight to the library where they accessed the secret passage to the sacred rooms. Bri and Sarah hesitantly went down the stairs to small hallway. There was a door there that was fairly obvious. Over in a dark corner there was another smaller door that would have been invisible if they hadn't been looking for it. Sarah opened the camouflaged door and entered the access code her mother had given her.

As they stepped through the door, Bri and Sarah were taken back. Bri stopped for a moment because she felt so disoriented. She felt a light buzzing in her head. For a moment she felt as if she were in another country in another time. Her body felt light and it seemed as if her heart and her head merged together into a place of absolute peace. She felt safer than she'd ever felt. She caught a whiff of a scent that smelled like a combination of lavender and something else she couldn't identify.

Sarah recovered first. She placed her hand lightly on Bri's arm. They exchanged a look of absolute connection with earth and the sacred room that they had stepped into.

Sarah said, "We can't absorb this now. Let's change out these artifacts and get out of here."

Bri nodded as she looked around. The walls appeared to be made of stone. One wall was completely covered with something like hieroglyphics. She knew from a trip to Egypt in college that ancient Egyptian monuments were once brilliantly painted. Now she was awed by the deep colors of gold, blue, purple, green, read and all the subtle variations.

Bri shook her head once again as she headed toward the long low tables at the front of the room. They were tables of elaborately carved wood and stone. In the center of the front of the room a niche was carved out of the stone wall. The sides were inlaid with jewels. Inside the niches was the statue of Inanna.

Bri and Sarah looked at each other - embarrassed by the inadequacy of the fake artifacts they had made. They only hoped that Victoria would be in too much of a hurry to pay attention.

Sara's mother had told them that only the Counsel got this close to the artifacts. They hoped Victoria would be disoriented by nerves, the amount of time it had been since she had been to a ceremony and by the fact she had never been this close to it.

Below the niche in the wall was an altar containing the book – *"The Goddess Documents."* It was thick with parchment pages. The cover was elaborately carved wood with a gold inset of the symbol for Inanna.

Once everything was in place, they said good night and crawled in bed to get a couple of hours of sleep.

Bri didn't think she'd be able to sleep at all. Protecting the Daughters of Inanna was foremost in her mind. But as soon as her head hit the pillow she was fast asleep.

The next morning she didn't feel tired at all, despite only getting a couple of hours of sleep.

"Are you ready?" Sarah asked Bri as the loaded into the house van.

"I supposed so," replied Bri.

"Come on you two, you should have it down by now, we've been going to the Center for months," said Kathy.

"I know, I guess I'm just a little slower than usual." Bri looked out the van window.

"Where's Jessie?" asked Sarah.

"She had a family emergency. She left the house about six this morning." Kathy climbed into the driver's seat. The rest of the women started off towards the Center.

As soon as they got to the Center, Sarah pulled Bri aside.

"Well, that's it. You're right it's definitely today. Convenient how Jessie had a family emergency today wasn't it?

"Let's go talk to the counselor now. We should get back as soon as possible." Bri looked around for the counselors.

A few minutes later, Bri and Sarah had discretely left the Center.

"Do you think anyone will notice we're gone?" asked Sarah.

"Kathy notices everything, but I don't guess it matters. They won't tell anyone until tonight. By then it will all be over."

They drove back towards the house in silence for a few minutes. They were obviously both lost in their own thoughts.

"So do you remember the final details of the plan we agreed to last night?" Bri finally asked.

"Yep, you really think it will work?" asked Sarah.

"I've got my fingers crossed," replied Bri.

A half hour later, they were installed in their hiding places in the library. As hard as it was for them, they remained still and silent. Nearly two hours had gone by before they heard anything.

The library door opened. Bri and Sarah heard the two women talking. One of them was definitely Jessie.

"I think you should increase my share, Victoria."

"Why's that Jessie?"

"Sneaking around Anne-Marie's office was dangerous."

"How else were we going to find out what the alarm codes were? It's just part of the job. You knew that this would be risky when we started. I'm just glad they had that schematic for the alarm installation. Now, we know exactly where Inanna's room is. I would hate to have to spend any more time fumbling around. Who knows when that Helen woman will be back?"

"Don't worry, she doesn't normally come back until early evening," Jessie replied.

"Yeah, I know, but we still need to keep moving."

It was quiet for a few minutes, while Jessie and Victoria fumbled for the entrance. Bri and Sarah waited a few more minutes in silence.

"So it should take about 10 minutes for them to get the book, statue and amulet and come back up, right?"

"Right... and how long will it take the police to get here? About 5 minutes? We certainly don't want them here too soon. That would expose too many secrets."

"So about 5 more minutes and we set off the alarm."

Bri and Sarah sat in nervous silence waiting for the appointed time. Then Bri got up and attempted to open the secret door to the underground entrance. She deliberately omitted the alarm codes. The watched the control panel as the silent alarm went off immediately.

Bri and Sarah hurried out of the room. Bri went to the back door and Sarah to the front. They wanted to be prepared in case Jessie and Victoria tried to get out.

After a few minutes, they heard sirens blaring down the street. Seconds later, Jessie and Victoria exited the house holding the counterfeit Daughters' treasures just as the police pulled up.

Bri acted like she had just arrived at the house. She was getting out of her car when the police pulled up. Diana and Anne-Marie pulled up at that moment too.

The commotion around the house went on for quite some time. While the police were questioning Jessie, Bri and Sarah pulled Diana aside and explained what they had done. Diana looked slightly amazed.

"But why are you and Anne-Marie back?" asked Sarah.

"We both had an intuition that we needed to be at the house now. So we left our meeting and came straight here." replied Diana.

"We Daughters have a sense of when our heritage is in Danger." Anne-Marie joined the small circle. "What you two did was very dangerous."

Bri and Sarah looked sheepish.

"Well give me a hug. You two saved the day." Bri and Sarah rushed into Anne-Marie's arms.

CHAPTER TWENTY-NINE

"You mean all the while Jessie and Victoria were planning to steal *"The Goddess Documents"* to sell them?" demanded Kathy.

The rest of the women had returned to the house. They were just getting the details of what had happened.

"Well, to sell the rights to publish them, for which they'd get a huge royalty."

"How did they think they'd get away with it? Wouldn't they have to explain where they got them?

"I don't understand that part, myself," replied Bri. Sarah just shrugged her shoulders.

Anne-Marie came into the room at that moment. "Don't you realize? Victoria has documentation of her maternal lineage, thanks to the Daughters, back close to a thousand years. She was planning to say it had been a well-kept family secret. She was going to say that in this information age nothing should be held back. We couldn't interfere without drawing too much attention to the organization."

The Trainees all shook their heads in wonder.

"What's going to happen to Jessie and Victoria now?" asked Kathy.

"They'll be charged with grand theft of the jewelry. Of course they couldn't resist when they saw the fortune in jewels our Councils have contributed. I don't suppose they will say much about the documents though. Besides who'd believe them without proof? They didn't even get out of here with their genealogies. I imagine they'll try to cut a deal with the District Attorney's office."

"But what if they go free? What about the documents?"

"We're adding additional protective measures. Victoria will be ruined in the publishing industry when they find out about the arrest. Lerner-Goode will have no doubt she was planning to deliver stolen goods. Her opportunity to profit will have passed. You can be sure they won't be caught around here any time soon."

CHAPTER THIRTY

The graduation ceremony was very beautiful and sacred. The statue and the book stood in their rightful places of honor. The ceremony room was opened. Daughters from all over the world attended. The room was filled with the light of the Goddess. The room was adorned with gold ornaments and stone carvings that glistened in the candlelight. The ceremony was the most amazing thing that Bri had ever experienced. She felt the love of all the Daughters streaming over her. Almost everyone cried, including Anne-Marie.

Although it had not been acknowledged at the ceremony, all of the Daughters knew about what had happened with Jessie and Victoria. After the ceremony, Bri and Sarah were flooded with congratulations and thanks from all of the Daughters.

Bri didn't get a chance to meet Sarah's mother, Eileen, until after the ceremony. They bonded immediately. Sarah's mother started treating Bri like a member of the family right away.

The banquet after the ceremony turned in to a celebration, not only of the graduation, but also of Bri and

Sarah's victory. They went to bed proud and exhausted that night.

As she lay in bed, Bri looked back over the last few months. They had been like a dream compared to the life she had come from. She was so happy she had chosen to follow her instincts and join the Daughters, instead of doing, the sensible thing.

The next day, while Sarah and Bri were packing up their things, Diana approached them.

"How would the two of you feel about apprenticing together? There's a young woman..."

ABOUT THE AUTHOR

Trudi White is an author and a Next Action Coach. She received her Masters Degree in Spiritual Psychology from the University of Santa Monica. In addition to, or perhaps in contrast of her personal spiritual journey she spent over 20 years in Corporate America. She considers herself to be grounded in the practical while having her head in the clouds.

Trudi's websites are: www.nextactioncoaching.com and www.thegoddessdocuments.com